## Where had everyone gone?

It was strange, Mother going off to work. There'd be this hurry while she and Daddy got ready to leave and then I'd be in the house alone.

By the end of August my confusion had worn off. I missed Drake—I even had a letter to him upstairs ready to mail—but things seemed okay in their new arrangement. I was looking forward to school, to band, to Keezie. Even the thought of piano lessons seemed a welcome change. Then it happened.

One Thursday morning I woke up to a room full of much too much light and a house empty of everyone but me. . . .

# The
# Stranger
# I Left Behind

George Ella Lyon

This novel was first published in hardcover under the title *Red Rover, Red Rover* by Orchard Books in 1989.

Copyright © 1989 by George Ella Lyon.

The lines of poetry quoted on pages 44-45 and 119 are from Gerard Manley Hopkins' "Spring and Fall—to a young child."

Published by Troll Communications L.L.C.

Reprinted by arrangement with Orchard Books, New York.

First paperback edition 1997.

Printed in the United States of America.

10 9 8 7 6 5 4 3 2 1

**Library of Congress Cataloging-in-Publication Data**
Lyon, George Ella (date)
[Red rover, red rover]
The stranger I left behind / George Ella Lyon.
— 1st Paperback ed.
p. cm.
Summary: When Sumi's brother leaves for boarding
school, her best friend moves away, her grandfather
dies, and her mother withdraws into grief,
Sumi finds herself facing the beginning
of adolescence alone and afraid.
ISBN 0-8167-4026-7 (pbk.)
[1. Family problems—Fiction.] I. Title.
PZ7.L9954St    1996
[Fic]—dc20        96-31631

*for*
ANN KILKELLY
*and*
MARTHA GEHRINGER
*the strength of your friendship*
*the light of your words*

*I was a very ancient twelve. My views at that age would have done credit to a Civil War Veteran. I'm much younger now than I was at twelve or anyway, less burdened. The weight of the centuries lies on children. I'm sure of it.*

FLANNERY O'CONNOR
*The Habit of Being: Letters*

# The Stranger
# I Left Behind

# 1

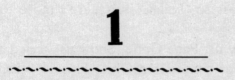

MEMORIAL DAY. My mother's whole family has gathered. We're headed over the mountains for a picnic at Steep Stone Park. Like always. Like always except we usually do this on the Fourth of July. We changed it this year because my grandfather died. We didn't want to follow the old pattern without him.

He died way last fall, before—well, before everything. I was just eleven then. In a way, Papa Gene's death was the beginning. Not the day he died, but all that came after his dying. I couldn't see it then, of course, any more than I could see what would happen to me.

Our picnic last year was the way it had always been. Only Papa Gene seemed different.

"It's awful to be old," he told my mother, as they sat at the shadiest picnic table in Steep Stone Park.

"You're not old," she said. "You can still touch

your elbows behind your back, can't you? And chin yourself with one hand?"

"I guess so, Ivalea. But there's more to it than that."

"Show us, Papa Gene! Show us!" cried a chorus of cousins come from Ohio, Florida, Virginia, for this one weekend, the Fourth of July, in the mountains.

"All right. Don't crowd me." He set down Ricky, who had climbed on his knee, and stood up, tall and thin, bones creaking. He turned up the sleeves of his khaki work shirt, rolled his shoulders once or twice and, easy as pie, touched his elbows bone to bone behind his back.

Applause and cries of "Wow! He did it!" "Betcha I can!" "Betcha you can't!"

Then all us kids and my mother followed him over to the monkey bars. Again he rolled his shoulders, but this time he bent at the waist, too, and laid the palms of his hands on the grass. Ricky and Brenda fell over trying to do the same. Papa Gene didn't notice. He straightened up, reached for the bar with his right hand, and slowly, slowly hoisted himself through the air. For a terrible minute I thought he wouldn't make it, but then, shaking with effort, he slid his chin across the bar.

More applause and "Wows!" and cries of "Lift me up! Let me!" but Papa Gene, the red draining from his face, just followed Mother back across the grass to the table.

"See," she insisted, "no old man could do that."

"Then I wonder," he said, "what in the world I could be."

# 2

THAT CONVERSATION WAS the only odd thing about the picnic. We cooked hamburgers as usual. Granny Reeb brought green beans, Mother brought baked beans; there were iced tea and watermelon and blazing meteors of marshmallows. And there was the Show.

When it was nearly dark, Papa Gene turned on his jeep headlights, and everybody pulled their blankets and folding chairs around the sheet of light like a stage. "Act quick," Papa Gene cautioned. "That's the only battery I have."

So my cousin Marvin did a magic trick (making his dad's handkerchief disappear in a false-bottomed hat), my cousin Brenda walked the length of the light on her hands, Roma yodelled, Tracy sang cartoon songs, I recited a poem, Drake played the recorder, and Tommy did an Abbott and Costello routine by himself.

The grown-ups clapped and laughed and slapped

at mosquitoes, and then it was over, hampers and coolers packed, chairs folded, car engines grinding into life.

Drake and Tommy rode in the jeep with Papa Gene, who headed up the caravan. Granny Reeb came right behind with Mother and Daddy and me. I was tired and sticky and happy, thinking how the white of my shorts was the brightest thing in the car. Then it happened. The taillights in front of us missed a curve; they left the road, bouncing haywire until the jeep came to rest against a cliff.

I know there were screams in the car, cries of "O my God!" but Daddy had laid on the horn so that's mostly what I heard. He eased off the road, motioning everyone to follow.

"Stay with your mother, Ivalea!" he warned and jumped out of the car.

But there was no holding Granny Reeb. Small as she is, she pushed Mother's hands away and shouldered her door open. The only trouble was the car was too close to the cliff. Seeing this, she turned and in a flash came over the seat, over me, and was out the back door and in the road.

By then Uncle Eb was coming up behind her, and Daddy had Papa Gene out of the jeep. Granny Reeb ran to him and my heart beat hard enough to hurt. He looked all right, but what about Drake?

"Stay in the car, Sumi," Mother ordered, sliding past the wheel. But Daddy had told *her* to stay in the car and she was climbing out. I waited a minute, then followed. I couldn't get near Papa Gene but I found Drake in front of the jeep, holding Tommy's head while he threw up.

"Are you okay? What happened?"

"I don't know. Tommy's head hit the dashboard. I think Papa Gene fell asleep."

"Tommy!" Aunt Sam came around the headlight. "O Lord, honey. Drake, give him to me."

In one motion, she slid between Drake and Tommy, catching the flap of her wrap-around skirt on the bumper.

"Can you see? Are you cut?" she kept asking between Tommy's retchings. A triangle of her slip shone white as the moon.

# 3

PAPA GENE said he *had* fallen asleep, and there was no real damage, though Uncle Eb and Aunt Sam sat up with Tommy all night.

"Don't let that boy go to sleep," Papa Gene insisted.

"You're one to talk," Granny Reeb said. "You get on to bed."

She acted like it was a joke—everyone did—but I could tell the grown-ups were shaken. Otherwise we wouldn't have all come back to Granny Reeb's. Otherwise the little kids couldn't have been helping themselves to cookies in the kitchen.

Finally, when Papa Gene had been snoring for half an hour—their bedroom was just off the living room—Mother said, "Do you really think he fell asleep?" I could tell how nervous she was. She kept taking down the gold roll of her hair and putting it up again.

"You could ask Drake," I suggested. "He was there."

Mother looked startled to see me, like she thought I was still on the mountain. "Where *is* Drake?" she asked.

"In the alley, I think. He and Marvin are setting off sparklers."

"Well, fetch him, would you, Sumi? You're right. He's just the one to ask."

So I made my way through the dark dining room, through the kitchen loud as a kindergarten, and out the back door. There wasn't much backyard, which was why the boys were in the alley. I could see the flash of sparklers around the garage.

"Drake, Mother wants you," I called. He let the sparkler fizzle out before he turned. Drake is tall like Daddy but has Mother's gold hair. Daddy's and mine is what they call dishwater blond.

"At your service," Drake said as he spun in the gravel. "Are we headed home?"

"Not yet. Mother wants to know if Papa Gene really fell asleep."

"Mmmmm."

"Did he?"

"Marv, I'll be right back," Drake said. "Here, catch!" He threw the matchbox.

"Did he?" I repeated.

"You come too. I only want to tell this once."

That didn't sound like Drake and it gave me the

creeps, but I followed him back into the house. In the kitchen Brenda and Roma were playing rummy at the table. Tracy and Ricky had a Candyland game on the floor. I wished I could sit down with them, could feel safe in that yellow light. But I wanted to hear what Drake said.

Back in the living room the grown-ups sipped coffee. Aunt Jenny was sewing name tags in shorts and Granny Reeb had taken up her tatting. Bent over the thread and shuttle, she drew her eyebrows together. Drake excused himself and walked in front of her to sit on the piano bench. That left me the footstool.

Drake didn't wait for the question. "What happened," he said, "at least what I *think* happened—you should ask Tommy, too—is everything was going along fine till pretty far up the mountain. We had the radio on WOWO and Tommy and I were singing along. Then all of a sudden Papa Gene reached over and turned it off. And he said to me, plain as day, 'Does it look foggy up here to you, Eb? I'm having the devil of a time making out the road.' "

"He called you Eb?" Granny Reeb asked.

Drake nodded.

"Then he wasn't solid in his mind," Aunt Debbie put in.

"Oh, Deb, hush," Uncle Hal told her.

"He didn't fall asleep!" Mother said. There was

a fierceness in her voice. "He's got to see a doctor. He's got to do it tomorrow!"

"I agree," Granny Reeb said, "but he won't. He's supposed to be in Lloyd County walking timber by nine o'clock."

"You won't let him go!" Mother challenged.

"No, and I won't let it snow this winter either."

"Mother . . ." She sounded like she might cry.

"Ivalea, calm down." Daddy stood up and put his hand on her shoulder. "We can see how he is in the morning. It's time to go and let your mother get to bed."

But Mother wouldn't go. After all the times she's said Daddy was good in a crisis—she says he knows how to calm people down because he's a vet—this time she wouldn't listen. She slept right where she sat on the cocoa-colored couch.

I don't know what she told Papa Gene in the morning, but it didn't get him to the doctor. It did, however, get her a day's ride in the jeep. That night she came home gritty with road dust and sawdust, smelling like the oily tools he hauled everywhere.

"Daddy will see the doctor tomorrow," she said, carrying in TV dinners. "And today he never once forgot who I was."

# 4

THE DOCTOR SAID Papa Gene's digestion was bad. When he heard what we'd eaten at the picnic, he said it was a wonder the jeep didn't veer across the road and tumble down the mountainside. What he prescribed was bland food, yeast cakes, and no driving after dark.

So the crisis passed and we got on with the summer. I was taking swimming lessons, trying to learn to dive without sending water up my nose.

"Just wear nose clips," Miss Jamison, the teacher, kept saying. Tall and muscled and gingerbread-brown, she looked like she could swim the English Channel. How could I tell her that nose clips scared me to death?

"I forgot mine," I said every day, feeling *coward* burned across my back like the X where my swimsuit straps crossed.

I'd always liked swimming though. And this year it had a special attraction. Mother said it was good over-all exercise and I'd decided I didn't want to be plump the rest of my life.

Drake's summer project was helping Papa Gene at the mill. Long before daylight the jeep would honk and I'd hear Drake across the hall stomping his feet into heavy shoes.

"Come on, son," Daddy would call. "Your grandfather's waiting."

In a minute the front door would slam and I'd go back to sleep.

By the time I got home from the pool, strawhaired and chlorine-eyed, Drake would be sitting at the piano practicing Schumann.

"How was the mill?" I'd ask. And he'd always answer:

"I can't move anything but my fingers."

Drake shoveled sawdust and lifted lumber but he wouldn't get near the saws. He's more afraid of cutting his fingers than I am of nose clips. He has reason, though. He's going to be a musician.

Both of us have taken piano ever since we could balance on the bench, but while I had to be bribed with coloring books and threatened with bed to practice, Drake had to be coaxed *away* from the keys.

At fourteen, he'd learned all our teacher could teach him and was leaving at the end of the summer for a private school, St. Talbott's in Philadelphia. "Careers are born there," Mrs. Conley had said.

I tried to be happy for him. I knew it was what
he wanted. Mostly, though, I felt sad. The fifteenth
of August, the day he would leave, weighed the
whole summer down.

My consolation was that I would still have Keezie,
my best friend since second grade. She'd seen me
through some pretty rough times—scarlet fever,
Ollie Traynor cutting off my pigtail—she'd help me
get along without Drake. We talked about this the
day I found out Drake was going.

"You'll have the house to yourself!" Keezie ex-
claimed when I told her over the phone.

"But I don't want it! Drake's not like Crazy Kate."

Crazy Kate is Keezie's little sister. Ever since she
threw up on Keezie's comic book collection Keezie
has been threatening to send her to a state home.

"No, but wait till he starts bringing in teenage
boys who pinch your arm and clomp around the
house like horses."

"Drake's friends aren't like that. Roy is the only
one who comes over, and he's kind of cute."

"Oh, Sumi!" Keezie moaned, disgusted. "You're
not going to get *interested* in them, are you? You
promised."

"No, no, except for Drake I think they're hopeless. I'm just saying that, for a boy, Roy is okay.
He's kind of all together, like a buckeye."

"Buckeyes are poison," she said.

"I know that. They're good luck, too. Anyway,

what I meant was he doesn't look like he's put together with rubber bands. You know, like Jimmy Steele."

I wished I could see into the narrow hall of Keezie's house as I said this. I knew she'd start imitating Jimmy's slow, disconnected walk.

Sure enough, there was static on the line as she jostled the phone.

We both laughed and left the subject of Drake and boys to go back to our usual phone work: imagining what sixth grade would be like.

We knew Mrs. Scott would be our teacher. Large and slow, she didn't promise much. But there were better things on the horizon. We'd both decided to start band, Keezie on trumpet and me on flute. Neither of us could play yet, but we were sure we'd be great at it. We saw ourselves, ninth graders a few years on, playing at pep rallies, marching in the Christmas parade, taking deep, brass-buttoned breaths and blasting them out into song. At least Keezie was going to blast.

"My dad said with a lip like this I'd be stupid not to play the trumpet," Keezie had told me. I didn't see anything odd about her lip, but that's the way her dad talks. "Of course he says it will sound better when I quit getting radio signals."

"What?"

"When I get the braces off."

"Oh, yeah." I don't have braces. I have "a slight

overbite, said to be perfect for the flute." Drake told me that, and when I relayed it to Keezie, she hooted.

"The orthodontic approach to the orchestra!"

I laughed so hard I got the hiccups and had to put down the phone and get a drink.

Anyway, much as I would miss Drake, I wasn't really worried about his going. I didn't know, of course, what it would feel like. Or that Papa Gene would die and everything would change. Until the end of that summer my world was as solid as the big old house I grew up in. I never thought how houses outlast the people they shelter, how what seems sure as the earth is the very thing you will lose.

# 5

DRAKE HADN'T been gone but a week when Mother declared she had gotten a job: receptionist for the new dentist in town.

"You don't need me to be here as much, Sumi," she explained at the dinner table. "And with Drake at St. Talbott's, the money will sure come in handy."

"Yes, it will," Daddy said, "but don't do it just for *that*, Ivalea. We can manage." I remember how he stopped eating a minute and just looked at her.

"I know, I know. But I guess I need—well, some distraction."

I wanted them to go on talking and let this news sink in. Now it would be not only Drake missing when I came in from school. Mother wouldn't be there either. . . .

"You don't, do you, Sumi?" Mother was asking. She looked at me intently.

"Don't what?" That sounded rude. "I'm sorry," I said. "I was daydreaming."

"Don't mind about the job?"

"Well, I'm not—"

"We'll all work together and it will be a good chance for you to learn how to cook and do wash—more independent things."

"Yes."

"I had to teach Drake about the perils of the laundry room before he left."

"I remember," I said, smiling. Drake had stood in the middle of the kitchen floor with clothes in heaps at his feet.

"She told me to separate them into white, dark, and bright," he had said. "But what about plaid? What about a white shirt with black sleeves? This pale blue thing with navy dots? And what about beige—it's not white, it's not dark . . ."

"Drake said if it was up to him he'd only wear black, white, and red," I told them.

"Very stylish," Daddy offered.

"Your brother is so stubborn," Mother said. "Witty, but stubborn."

"And I don't know where he gets it," Daddy added.

They laughed.

"Me neither," Mother said. "I have no earthly idea."


IT WAS strange, Mother going off to work. There'd be this hurry while she and Daddy got ready to leave and then I'd be in the house alone. Sometimes when the door closed and the car started I'd console myself thinking Drake would be back in the afternoon. Then I'd remember Drake was gone, too. He wouldn't be home till Christmas.

But by the end of August my confusion had worn off. I missed Drake—I even had a letter to him upstairs ready to mail—but things seemed okay in their new arrangement. I was looking forward to school, to band, to Keezie. Even the thought of piano lessons seemed a welcome change. Then it happened.

One Thursday morning I woke up to a room full of much too much light and a house empty of everyone but me.

# 6

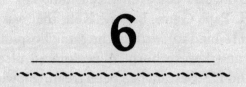

THERE WAS A NOTE on the back of an envelope propped on my dresser:

> *Sumi,*
> *They took your grandfather to the hospital at four this morning. Your mother is with Granny Reeb. Since they may need you, I let you sleep.*
> *Call me at work.*
>
> *Daddy*

My heart started knocking before I even read the note, and by the time I got to the end I could feel the fear kicking in my stomach too.

That's why I didn't help myself to the coffee Daddy had left plugged in and why I ruined the pot, so that the first thing the church ladies had to do that night was send somebody out for a new one. They had brought the church urn, but said we wouldn't be wanting forty cups just yet.

The house was choked with these women I'd said hello to once a week ever since I could talk. Because he died. Papa Gene. Eugene Kell, that was his full name. He bled to death in the same hospital where Drake and I were born. A perforated ulcer, they said. And Dr. Bascam had been treating it with yeast cakes.

So he died, doing just what they'd prescribed. What would Drake say about that?

Drake was crazy about Papa Gene. They'd gotten close when he'd helped out at the sawmill, running messages, learning what he could. I thought we could talk about it when he came back for the funeral, and then I wouldn't feel so alone. Because I did. All those people crawling over the house and it still empty. Everything deserted like that morning I woke up. *Drake*, I wanted to say, *something's funny. I'm scared*.

But Drake, when he finally got here, was part of the change. He had on his uniform—gray pants, navy blazer with a school crest slapped above his heart—and was stark white except for a nick on his cheek which said he had started shaving. He smelled different too. Partly his school and the train, partly whatever shaving lotion he used. He hugged me at the door and I wanted to tell him everything, but the same silence hung on him that was over all of us. Used to be they hung crepe on houses where there'd been a death. Now it's just silence. All the voices of women peeling Saran Wrap off asparagus casseroles can't touch it. And the low rumble of men in the living room might as well be thunder in the next county.

So, though Drake was here for three nights and two days, we never had a real conversation. All our cousins poured in, which meant when Drake did come out of the cloud for a minute he was off with Tommy or Marvin. Then, after the funeral, he had to go back to Bristol to catch the train. We didn't even get to take him. Uncle Eb and Aunt Sam live in Dungannon so they dropped him off on the way home.

Right after he left even the empty words went out of the house. Keezie came over for a while, but we both felt too awkward to talk. Then I was alone with Mother and Granny Reeb. Nobody cried, nobody wailed. They spoke in flat voices about what had to be done. When they got around to money, Mother asked me to leave.

I went up to my room and took out my letter to Drake. It seemed stupid, all about how kids at the pool made fun of my name. So what? I'd have to start another letter. I'd write about waking up that morning and how terrible it felt. I'd write all I'd wanted to tell him. He'd understand. There wouldn't be a funeral between us when he sat down to read.

# 7

SO I GOT some stationery, a notebook to bear on, lay across the bed, and fell asleep. When I woke up it was drizzling. Daddy had come home, I remember, because I thought how reassuring his voice felt. I couldn't hear it exactly, but the vibrations coming from downstairs had deepened.

Still groggy, I went across the hall to Drake's room. Now that he'd been home it smelled like oranges again. Wherever he goes Drake leaves little stacks of orange rind. Not heaps, stacks, fitted together. "Like cairns," he told Mother, "roadside monuments."

"But cairns are made out of stone," she said. "And this isn't the roadside." Then she bought him a metal wastebasket covered with crests of baseball teams. It didn't work.

The first few days after we had taken Drake to school I liked going into his room. I'd sit on his bed and pretend he'd be back as soon as his piano lesson was over or Wig was fed. Wig is our cat. But by the end of the week all the comfort of that had leaked away.

Because he had just been home, there was a trace of energy in his room, like dust stirred when a car has driven by. It was so lonely I started to cry, sitting on his bed, running my hand over the lumpy covers. I felt guilty crying about Drake instead of Papa Gene. Then I thought about Granny Reeb going into their bedroom, looking at Papa Gene's clothes, knowing he'd never be back. And I cried that much harder. It seemed like I couldn't stop. Everything in Drake's room—the maple bed, the desk with his autographed baseball, the bare place where his record player had been—everything looked lost. It was as if Drake, in going, had cut all the strings that held things to him, that made them matter. I went back to my room.

Wig was on the bed. I was glad to see her. She'd been hiding ever since the women came with food that first night. *Now a dog*, I said to Drake in my mind, *a dog would have been fawning all over those strangers, sniffing dishes. Whereas a cat*—I looked at Wig, her gray stripes mottled with orange underneath—*a cat has integrity*.

Drake would have had some smart reply to that, like "You call it integrity because she deserted us at the crucial moment?" He doesn't like cats on principle. "But Wig is an exception," he'd said, after

I'd had her a couple of weeks. "Look at her coat. How often do you see a torbie?" I bet him fifty cents he'd made it up.

I lost, too. *Torbie* is just as much a word as *toaster*. It's a cat breeder's term which means half tabby and half tortoiseshell. That's part of my trouble with Drake: I never know whether he's leading me by the hand or pulling my leg. Most of my life I've followed in his wake like a one-person raft towed by a twelve-seater. Family, neighborhood, school: Drake chose our path through the rapids. And kept an eye out to see if I'd come loose or was trapped in a whirlpool. And I looked ahead to him to see which way to lean. So that's how you climb a tree or take swimming lessons. How you have measles.

But how do you act when at age eleven you've become an only child? When there's a death in the family? Not a death you visit, but one you have to live with? I didn't know, and Drake wasn't there to tell me. He couldn't have anyway. It wasn't his life.

# 8

I DID WRITE that letter, sometime the next week, three versions of it. *Dear Drake*, I started out, *you don't know what it's like around here.*

> *There used to be two of us and two of them. But now with Granny Reeb always on their minds, it's like there's three of them and one of me—*

but that sounded like I thought it was his fault. He'd always said, "As long as we have a balance we don't have to worry. There's two of them and two of us, see?" I tried again:

> *Dear Drake,*
> *How long do you suppose it takes for things to get back to normal after somebody dies? Everyone's acting so strange. I don't know what to do.*

That didn't sound right either. It would have been one thing to walk across the hall and talk to him about it or go downstairs and interrupt his piano exercises. But written down it was different. I tried another approach:

*Dear Drake,*
 *So you've started shaving and getting dressed up every day. What's it like? Do you have raw oysters for breakfast? Do you get to practice all you want?*

I couldn't go on like that, though. The trouble was, none of my letters helped me envision Drake on the other side of them. I didn't know where his post office was. I'd seen his room, but only when it was gray and empty and Drake was the only room-mate who'd arrived. I didn't know which desk was his, how to picture him. I was afraid he'd be opening the letter and some big guy across the room would say, "Hey, who's that from?" and he'd shrug and say, "My kid sister again," and put the paper back in its envelope. It wouldn't be Drake shrugging so much as his school blazer. Whether he had it on or not.

MOST DAYS Mother came home about four o'clock, but sometimes she ran late, stopping by to see Granny Reeb or running to the store for her.

Then I'd get a call with instructions on what to start for dinner.

I liked that. I'd been learning to cook in Girl Scouts. Of course, you can't eat scrambled eggs, campfire beans, and s'mores every night, so Mother taught me to fix other things. It wasn't a big step. I'd been helping out in the kitchen for a while.

Besides, there's some fun in doing things for your parents, in thinking how they'll come home tired and you'll have a hot meal for them. But Mother was more than tired. If her job distracted her from grief during the day, coming home must have brought it all back.

I don't mean that she cried. Even Granny Reeb didn't do much of that, at least not where I could see. Mother just seemed weighed down. But she wouldn't sit and let me do for her. If I had dinner ready, she'd start cleaning something while I put it on the table—wiping crumbs off the toaster or scrubbing the sink. Daddy would pour them both coffee and "doctor" hers. That's what he calls making it too sweet for anybody but her to drink.

If Mother got home on time, before Daddy, I'd come down from wherever I was reading (sometimes upstairs, sometimes in the elm tree) to see if I could help start dinner. But I could no more help her than you could help a whirlwind. She turned a potato twice in her hands and it was peeled. She opened the refrigerator and *bam!* there were three pots simmering on the stove. She'd always been efficient but this was different. This was vengeance.

I didn't know then that grief could make you mad. I just knew that Mother was gone a lot and that, when she was home, she wasn't really Mother. She never joked anymore. She never put her arm around me. I wasn't sure she'd done that before, but it used to *feel* like she did. And I missed it. I missed her. But when she came home, I'd have to get out of her way.

And I'd have to be cheerful. If I so much as frowned or forgot to have any expression for a while, she'd say, "Don't be sad, honey. I can stand it from anybody but you." Or, if the day was wound tighter, "Just perk up, Sumi. We can't have any long faces around here."

Nobody said How are you. Nobody talked about missing Drake. Maybe I had to miss him enough for everybody. We'd be eating spaghetti or hash or meat loaf and I'd think how Drake used to get called down for humming at the table. He didn't do it on purpose. There was just so much music in his head that some leaked out. He and I had a joke about it. I'd try to keep him talking so he wouldn't hum. Every time Mother or Daddy began a long speech I'd look for a way to bring Drake in. Not until he left did I wonder if they'd noticed.

I wanted to write Drake about this, about Mother's fierce cooking and her job, about Daddy looking kind of lost. I did write him. But every time, once the letter was finished, I thought it sounded stupid. Surely I could do better. Maybe I could even write something so good that Drake would want to come home.

# 9

SCHOOL STARTED the day after Labor Day. I was so glad to see the classroom, to be somewhere that wasn't smothered with funeral flowers. I just sat and stared. Everybody had grown. The boys were louder than usual, the girls quieter. Jimmy Steele had braces. Rose Fletcher had a bra. You couldn't tell, but she boasted about it in the bathroom.

It took Mrs. Scott three tries to get through the roll. Keezie turned around in her seat and raised her eyebrows. Lucky for us, our last names are next door in the alphabet so we always wound up neighbors whether the teacher let us choose or not.

"It's going to be a long year," Keezie's look said, and sure enough, it took Mrs. Scott till Friday just to get the books passed out. By then I was ready for a nap.

Mother had other plans. Saturday she and Granny Reeb were taking me shopping. Ordinarily

Granny Reeb wouldn't have come along, but Mother thought she needed to get out of the house. This meant I had two clothes critics—three if you count the ever-eager clerk.

Summer had not left me bronzed and curvy, as the suntan lotion ads implied, but at least I was too tall to be directed to the Chubby rack. I found a few things to try on and went back to the dressing room.

"There's a girl hidden in there," I heard Granny Reeb tell Mother on the other side of the curtain. I thought she meant some girl changing in the next booth. "Any year now she is going to come out."

She was talking about me! My ears burned. I'd always been teased for being chubby, but that was a kid-thing. It would disappear when I started to grow up. Now, looking at my body in the dingy dressing-room light, I knew I wasn't a kid anymore. And the struggle to zip up the size eleven dress told me I wasn't getting skinny either. I was fat. That's what Granny Reeb meant.

"Do you need help, Sumi?" Mother called.

"No, no, I've got it." I pushed the curtain aside. The dress was teal blue and it fit like frog skin.

"Oh, my," Mother said. "Not that. Try the sailor-collared one."

"Okay." I hoped it was a thirteen.

"Whatever else you get or don't get," Granny Reeb said, "that child needs a brassiere."

"Oh, no!" Mother protested. "Sumi's only eleven. She's much too young."

"Not judging from the fit of that dress."

"That's just baby fat. I'll make her wear an undershirt," Mother promised.

I waited in the dressing room mortified.

"Baby fat in some mighty predictable places," Granny Reeb declared. "I'd open my eyes if I were you."

But Mother didn't. We took the blue-striped sailor dress and an autumn-leaf colored skirt and blouse I liked a lot. We also bought anklets and undershirts.

"I don't believe it," Granny Reeb said, as the cashier rang up the sale.

"Are you getting tired?" Mother asked. "I guess it's time for some lunch."

"I am *not* tired," Granny Reeb answered, measuring out her words. "But if you will take me home now, I will make us a little lunch."

I wasn't sure how they could argue without saying the words, but I knew they were doing it. As quickly as possible we found the car and drove to her house.

Granny Reeb made chicken-salad sandwiches (with the crusts trimmed off) and spiced tea. It was still hot outside but her house was cool and the sun on her white enameled table dazzled my eyes.

When Papa Gene was alive they ate only breakfast in the kitchen. The other meals were at the big table in the dining room. Now she never ate in there. If Daddy and Mother and I came to supper we'd all squeeze around the kitchen table. "I'm sorry," she'd tell us, "but that room is too empty for me." She'd wave her hand at the dining room.

I knew what she meant. Her whole house felt empty. Or too filled with absence, like Drake's room. I tried to write Drake about it that night, tried to capture the morning, including their argument at the store. But all that came across was I was mad at Granny Reeb for thinking I was fat.

# 10

---

~~~~~~~~~~~~~~~~~~~~~~~~~~~~~~~

FORGET IT, I said to myself. Why would Drake
want to come back when all you can write are these
whiny letters? Maybe I'd do better trying to tell
him about school. If home was strange, school was
like Mars.

*Dear Drake,*

*Do you remember Cathy Blanchard? Very
pretty, in my class, lives in the old Roper house.
Well, she is smart, always has been, and the only
person I know whose math looks like script.*

*Today she told Mrs. Scott she didn't know where
Venezuela is.*

*"I've heard of it, Mrs. Scott," she purred. "Is it
somewhere near Greece?"*

*She shook her head to show off her auburn hair.
I'll bet she could locate Caracas.*

*I was so put out I wouldn't walk home with*

*her. I came through Death Valley instead. Hardly any girls in my class will do that now.*

Death Valley is a washed-out cornfield which, for some reason, is about fifteen feet lower than the rest of Talmidge, where my school is. The paved street ends at one side and takes up on the other. To get down you have to tilt from rock to root, and coming up you have to use your hands a little. I don't go when it's muddy, but otherwise I like it. Better than hugging the road. Drake always went that way. Till I was in the fourth grade we walked it together.

*And Cathy's not the only one,* I wrote Drake:

*Most of the sixth-grade girls act like they got swimmer's ear over the summer and chlorine bleached their brains. Angie Sizemore paints her fingernails through English class, and every time Mrs. Scott calls on Jan Lewis, she says, "Ask Jimmy Steele. I bet he knows."*

*Jimmy might know but he's usually half asleep. That leaves me and Keezie with all the answers. "Are your lights always on upstairs?" Dale Rowlett asked me the other afternoon. What do they expect me to do—go around in the dark? If it weren't for Keezie, I'd think I was crazy.*

*Did girls start acting like this when you were in sixth grade? They think it makes boys like them,*

*I know. Does it? And what good is that, if they like somebody you're only pretending to be?*

I think I would have mailed that letter, because it was more like talks we had, except at supper the night I would have finished it, Mother read us a letter from Drake. I can't quote it exactly but the big news was that he had found a girlfriend, Wendy something-or-other, who goes to Glenwood, a girl's school nearby.

I felt kind of hurt—well, maybe more than *kind of*—but that's not the worst of it.

"Is Glenwood a preparatory school, too?" I asked, trying to act positive.

"No," Mother said. "It's more of a finishing school."

"What's that?"

"Oh, a place where girls learn the social graces. Academics, too, but they're scaled down. The emphasis is on cultivating fine manners—you know, a little music, a little dance—"

"But what if a girl was serious about music, like Drake?"

"It wouldn't be the school for her."

"What school would?"

"I don't know right off."

"But that's not fair!"

"Sumi," Daddy said, "how do you know this Wendy person has any interest in music at all?"

"I don't think that's the point, Charles," Mother put in.

"Well, if she doesn't care for music, what does Drake want with her? She can't understand him!"

Struggling to keep back tears, I got up and left the table. *Drake, how could you?* I thought all the way up the stairs. I pounded my pillow, then hugged it close. *He gets prepared and she gets finished*, I thought. *Cathy Blanchard. Venezuela. I can't stand it. And Drake's not going to want to hear from me, his kid sister who still answers in class.* "I hate this!" I said to the little stuffed tiger Drake had sent. His school mascot. "I hate you." And I did my best to rip its striped head off. It didn't give, and in a second I felt stupid. Tearing up tigers wouldn't help anything. I'd call Keezie.

"Guess what?" Keezie said, before I could begin.

"What?"

"We're moving."

# 11

"YOU CAN'T *do* that," Daddy said to Mother as she was trying single-handedly to move Granny Reeb's couch.

"Well, *you* can't do it. Not with your back." Daddy has disk trouble.

"I know that, Ivalea. That's why I hired Josh and his boy. They'll be here in a minute if you'll just hold on."

We were standing in the middle of Granny Reeb's once-perfect living room, now a maze of furniture and boxes. She was moving to an apartment.

"We'll have a cup of coffee while we wait," Granny Reeb said, appearing in the dining-room doorway. Moving day or not, she looked neat and calm, a small round woman with a cap of gray-brown hair.

"But I packed the cups," my mother said.

"I have some paper ones," her mother answered. "Come out to the kitchen."

So we did.

As we sat at the table, Daddy stared into his coffee like a gypsy gazing in a crystal ball. I was wondering whether it was the past or the future he saw, when suddenly he looked up.

"A lot of years in this house, Mrs. Kell. A lot of life."

"Charles, please," Mother said, darting a look at Granny Reeb, then at him. "Not now."

For a minute we sat silent.

"I believe I left out the tin of butter cookies," Granny Reeb announced. "Would you see if they're on the stove, Sumi?"

This house is Granny Reeb's world, I thought. We can't move her out.

But we had to. The house was too big and it cost too much. If her heart couldn't be moved, well, she'd just have to do without.

Keezie had said the same thing about moving. "The order comes down and you're transferred. Nobody asks how you feel, much less how your kids feel." That was a sort of death too.

I had told Mother about it one night while we were folding laundry. "Keezie's moving. Her dad's been promoted to a hospital in Williamson."

"Oh dear. When?"

"Before Thanksgiving." It was already mid-October.

"Hmmmm," she said, smoothing one of Daddy's

undershirts. She had a system of folding Daddy's one way and Drake's another so we wouldn't mix them up. Now it didn't matter. "That'll be hard on you, Sumi, but I think I can see a bright spot. Sometimes it's not good to rely too much on one friend. Without Keezie you'll be forced to branch out."

My turn to say "Hmmm."

"Always look for an advantage, honey. Lessons come hard sometimes, but they do come."

*But I don't* want *this lesson*, I thought. What I said was, "Keezie will still be my best friend."

"Maybe so, but she won't be here. You'll need friends close by."

"We've already promised to write."

"Speaking of writing, when do you plan to send that brother of yours a letter?"

"Any day now," I told her. "I've got one started."

As I folded bath towels I thought of the letters folded upstairs, with one edge closed and three open just like the towels. What would happen if you had hand-letters and bath-letters, guest-letters and dish-letters, if every time you got wet, you had to dry off on words? I could have told Drake about that. Or Keezie. I could still have told her but she seemed distant now that she was going away.

Have you ever noticed how, when someone is leaving, you feel their absence before they're really gone? How sometimes it makes you pick a fight, sometimes just be silent? The silence is what happened with Keezie and me. And, though we promised to write, she warned me that letters were not her line.

"I can't talk on paper," she said. "If I could draw you something or send you a message in math . . ."

"If you did I'd never decipher it." We laughed at that. Math is not one of my gifts.

So I started trying harder to write to Drake. Not on paper so much as in my head. And even though I didn't mail these messages, Drake sent one to me. It came with a birthday present. I turned twelve on the seventeenth.

*Sumi*, said the note penciled on yellow paper and tucked into a paperback book:

*I dare you to read this. It's our first book for sophomore English. Doesn't make sense till you quit expecting it to be like anything else.*

*Your buddy,*
*Drake*

The book was white with black letters stacked on the front like Roman numerals. *As I Lay Dying*, it said. William Faulkner. Seemed like I'd heard of him. I tried a few pages. From what I could tell, it was all about some man sawing. Maybe it reminded Drake of the mill.

Anyway, Drake's note was what I wanted to read.

Since it was so short, I tried to make it say more than it did. "I dare you . . ." Did that mean he thought I couldn't do it? Did he think I believed all books should be alike? And somehow his signing "Your buddy" bothered me. He used to call me Buddy sometimes, but then we were little kids.

Here I had word from Drake but I couldn't enjoy it. Like my letters, it didn't bring him closer; it made him seem farther away. I flipped through the book, reading chapter headings. They were character names. I turned to the one called "Addie" and skimmed some pages. Words, she said, were "just a shape to fill a lack." It gave me chills. That's exactly what I felt in writing to Drake. It was true and Addie knew it. I closed *As I Lay Dying* and put it under my bed. I didn't want to read Drake's gift at all.

# 12

ALMOST THANKSGIVING. Keezie had gone. Drake was too far away to come home for just three days. Our first holiday without him and Papa Gene. The dread was as heavy as the turkey. Frozen solid.

At school Cathy and I were chosen to decorate the board—Cathy because her lettering's so good and me because I love chalk. When I was little I wanted one wall of my room to be a chalkboard so I could draw letters and numbers as big as me. And so I could use colored chalk. I practiced on my little slate rubbing the side of the chalk across the cloudy blackness, two or three colors to make a blend. So I got to feather Cathy's turkeys.

The class was insulted by the whole thing. Didn't Mrs. Scott notice that we weren't eight years old anymore? She taped construction-paper leaves to the windowpanes: red, yellow, orange. She gave us stars for extra reading. Now the turkeys. I didn't care. I got to play with chalk.

Brown and orange and a little purple for the body, brown and red for the feathers, banded with white and green. I finished before Cathy's pilgrim was ready, and she wanted to leave her letters white, so I turned my attention to the bookshelf under the blackboard. It held old ragged textbooks and examination copies of new ones. I pulled out *Adventures in Reading* or something like that. It opened to a full-page photograph of a girl looking out the window into some great red-leaved tree. A poem was printed over it.

Margaret, are you grieving
Over Goldengrove unleaving?

It made me shiver.

Leaves, like the things of man, you
With your fresh thoughts care for, can you?

The classroom was too hot.

Ah! as the heart grows older
It will come to such sights colder
By and by, nor spare a sigh
Though worlds of wanwood leafmeal lie,

The words didn't make any sense. Wet sweaters steamed on the radiator and my stomach closed on lunch like a fist.

And yet you will weep and know why.

I sat down. It wasn't even my desk. It was Rose Fletcher's, but she was home sick. Several kids were absent. I thought I must be getting it, whatever it was. I laid the book on top of the shelf and put my head on my arms. The shiny smell of the pencil groove hurt my nose.

Then *grring!* the electric bell started a frenzy. I sat up to the slap of books, the stampede of feet. Cathy, her forefinger in a wet rag, was tracing the outline of her turkey, removing smudges. The pilgrim stood clear.

"I'll have to color him tomorrow," I told her. "I don't feel so good."

"I can stay late and do it," she offered. "What if you're not here tomorrow?"

I hadn't considered that. "Okay." I started to say something to the teacher but she must have gone down the hall. "Will you explain to Mrs. Scott?"

"Sure, Sumi. You better get going. You look a little green."

So I picked up *Advanced Fun with Numbers* and my Nifty notebook and left.

How could you have Advanced Fun? I wondered,

walking down the dark hall and out into gray light. How could you have fun with numbers, period? I knew my father did. And Keezie loved them. She'd smile at the quick columns she drew with her mechanical pencil. It looked fast and effortless when she did it, like the tatting from Granny Reeb's shuttle. And Keezie solved the problems just as easily. She'd hold her breath a second, her hand with the clear yellow pencil poised up by her ear, then Ah! the breath came out, the hand came down, and it was done.

Not me. I don't mind simple stuff. But the longer the distance between the start of the problem and its answer, the more confused I get. At the end what I come up with is like the phrase in a game of Gossip, transformed by all those whisperings.

I sure missed Keezie. We always brought our lunches and sat on the sidewalk by Wade's Alley to eat. She was so funny. "An egg and olive sandwich," she'd say, taking the wax paper off like she was defusing a bomb. "That woman wants to poison me!"

Mostly we laughed while we ate, reviewing the morning, but after that we walked, and the motion, or full stomachs, or deeper breathing, made us serious.

We talked about war and outer space—Keezie's going to be a scientist. We even talked about God.

"I'm a Presbyterian," she said one day, "but God's not a Presbyterian."

"That's a relief," I told her. "My family's Methodist."

"No, I mean really, do you think God is even Christian?"

"Not for a lot of the world."

"Most of it," she insisted. "So what about us?"

I had thought about that question too. "What if God appears in whatever shape you can take Him? I mean, whatever your culture can accept?"

"So Buddha and Jesus are the same?"

"Well, sort of," I said.

"What about missionaries then? What about the Crusades?" Keezie's hands flew up and she pretended to tear at her short frizzy brown hair.

"I'll admit that's a problem."

She wrinkled her nose and laughed. This was the corner we always came to, in our conversation as well as our walk.

"You can't solve the problems of the world on a lunch hour," one of us would say, and then the bell would ring or we'd go get Mallo-Cups, only to continue our talk that night on the phone.

Boy, did I miss her! I couldn't think of a soul in my class who thought more about church than what to wear.

After Keezie moved, I started eating in the cafeteria. That was easier, anyway, with Mother working. The rest of the lunch hour I stood around the playground with Ann Jones and Libby Miller. They came from poor families and didn't have makeup to reapply or boyfriends to whisper about. We must have talked, but I don't remember a scrap of what we said, gathered there just to keep from being alone.

# 13

WE GOT THROUGH Thanksgiving. A smaller turkey. No leaf in the dining-room table. But we had the spiced peaches Drake loves and Granny Reeb made Papa Gene's favorite, scalloped oysters. "We'll eat them for him," she said. "Gene always claimed that Advent began with the first bite of scalloped oysters."

Advent. The season of waiting. This year it wasn't Christmas I x'd across the calendar toward. It was December twenty-first, Drake's homecoming. And whenever our minister talked at church about "having a burden on your heart," I thought when Drake came home it would be lifted, the way someone meeting you at the door takes the heavy groceries.

The days grew shorter. That had never bothered me before, but being closed up in the house earlier every day was too much like being shut up in myself. I'd look out my window at lights going on in other houses and think of all those walls, all the rooms and doors and closets, set up against the grid of streets, and the mountains around us, an endless chain of walls. Drake would come home on the darkest day of the year. Then things would get brighter.

I READ a magazine article once called "Taking Charge" or something like that. It was all about planning for changes in your life and how you should make sure the big shifts happen one at a time. For example, don't make a major change soon after someone has died. You see how stupid that is. Papa Gene died and Granny Reeb had to sell the house. Then it said, don't change jobs and move at the same time. Sure. Keezie's dad could accept his promotion and commute two hundred miles a day. Whoever writes these things forgot about "It never rains but it pours."

Well, I didn't have to worry about grown-up things like widowhood and jobs. It was the growing-up things I was stuck with, and I didn't even know what they were. Oh, I knew I would get breasts and hair—I was even starting to—but there was more to it. I'd seen the mysterious ads in Granny Reeb's *McCalls*, a beautiful lady in a cloudlike dress with the inscription "Modess because . . ." Because what? I had no idea.

Then one day after playing basketball in P.E. I noticed it—a rusty stain. When I told Mother that night she said, "My, my." And then, "Don't worry, Sumi. It's normal." Normal? How?

"But it looks like blood," I told her.

"It's all right," she said.

I thought maybe I'd hurt myself somehow playing so hard. I really liked basketball.

A week later, the same thing. I felt ashamed. Everybody knew you weren't supposed to soil your underwear. That night I rolled up the culprit and shoved it to the back of my drawer.

But I couldn't keep it there. December tenth in the middle of the night I woke up with pain radiating from somewhere below my waist. I sat up in bed, turned on the light. The room tilted. Some virus, I thought. I'd better get to the bathroom.

I was wearing red clown pajamas. They were babyish and too small, but it was cold and we hadn't bought new ones yet. I climbed out of bed shivering and all at once realized I was wet. How could that be? I'd *never* wet the bed, not in my remembrance. Could I have thrown up—or something worse— without knowing? I looked at the sheet and my heart caught in my chest.

There was a circle of blood where I'd been lying, an iris staring from the white eye of the sheet. I took off my pajamas bottoms, the elastic catching at my ankles. They were dark with the blood that trickled down my legs.

The chill brought a clench of pain and more

blood. What was wrong? Could I be dying? Tears came too as I went down the hall to Mother and Daddy's room.

Their door has a mirror on it, on the hall side. In the half-light from my room I thought I saw my mother coming out. *She knows something's wrong,* I thought. *She woke up.* But it was only me, looking like a collision victim, with my ruffled flannel clown top and naked, bloody legs.

"Mother," I whispered into the hot smoky darkness of their room. No answer.

"Mother!" Louder, trying not to cry.

Daddy rolled over and snored. I walked around to her side of the bed, touched her shoulder, naked except for the lace strap of her nightgown.

"Mother!"

Her dark eyes opened wide and stared for a minute like she'd never seen me before. Then she sat up.

"Sumi! What's wrong?"

"I'm sick," I said. "I don't know. There's all this blood."

"Shhhhhh," she whispered, lifting back the covers, climbing out of bed. "Let's go into the bathroom."

On the way, she took Daddy's robe from the bedpost. The white terry cloth could have gone around her twice.

The bathroom was much brighter than my room. I cringed.

"Oh, Sumi," Mother said, worry waking her, "tell me where it hurts."

"Right here," I said, laying my palm over my navel.

"Does it help to rub it?"

"Some."

"I'll fix you a hot-water bottle," she said.

"But Mother, shouldn't we go to the hospital?"

For a minute we stood there, her in her double layer of night clothes, me half naked.

"No, honey," she said finally. "We need to get some sleep. We'll see how you are in the morning."

"What's going on, Ivalea?" We had waked Daddy.

"It's all right, Charles. Sumi doesn't feel well is all."

Doesn't feel well? "Daddy—" I started.

"Sumi," Mother interrupted, "you wash off and leave the washcloth soaking in cold water. There's some aspirin in the drawer there. I'm going downstairs to fill this." She held up the floppy bottle. On the way down she took a detour to their room and I heard her and Daddy whispering.

After I'd washed and taken the aspirin I went to my room and put on clean pajamas. Then I remembered the sheet. Maybe I should put a hand towel between my legs like a bandage. I was back in the bathroom when Mother reached the top of the stairs.

"My sheet's all bloody," I told her.

"Why don't you sleep with us then, honey?"

"Okay."

I'd done that before when I was sick. It was comforting. But not this night.

Mother put a bath towel down for me to lie on and I felt ashamed and afraid. Why weren't they worried? If Drake had waked up bleeding, we'd be at the emergency room by now. What was different? I kept hurting and shaking, trying not to cry, not to bleed on them. Most of the night I lay awake, tensed against what was happening, my parents on either side like live walls.

# 14

DADDY WAS GONE by the time we woke up. The first thing Mother did was run me a bath. "This'll make you feel a lot better," she said.

It did. In the deep, warm water I began to relax and it felt good to wash. Strange, though, to be bathing in the morning. I opened the shutters and let sunlight splash in the tub.

I was just drying off when Mother came in the door. "Oh, Sumi, close those shutters."

"Mother, we're upstairs. No one can see."

"Maybe not now, but they can at night. You don't want to get in the habit of bathing like that."

I thought of how she bathed, with the shutters closed and not even a light on.

"I have something for you," she said.

She was carrying a blue box and what looked like a garter belt. She showed me how to put it on. Then she opened the box. I knew what was in it because once I had found such a box in her closet. But I had been sneaking to look for Christmas presents, so I couldn't ask her about it. I'd heard of women taking beauty rests and thought the pads might go over your eyes.

"Here," she said, taking one out. "This will fix you right up. The blood will only last about a week. You're growing up, Sumi! I didn't expect my little girl to be growing up so soon."

"But what is it?"

Mother looked pained. "It's a healthy sign. Don't you worry. Just change the pads often and keep extra clean."

How could it be healthy to bleed? To feel sick as I had the night before? I was lost. But there was a feeling between Mother and me—strong as a magnetic field—that said, "Don't ask any more." So I didn't.

Except for meals and school, I stayed in my room that week. I felt awkward, afraid to move and give myself away. It didn't occur to me to ask anybody at school about it. I wasn't close to anyone but Keezie and she was gone. Instead, I was panicked that somebody would notice, especially in the bathroom. Some of the stalls had no doors, and on others the locks were broken. There was no place you could count on privacy. And the person who opened the door on you might be in the eighth grade or the first.

Ordinarily I spent the time between school and supper outside, riding my bike or playing in the neighborhood. Not now. And I quit writing letters to Drake. There was no point in even trying to tell him about this.

I felt exiled. Right there in my own room with my parents close by, I felt cut off by this shameful secret. Mother hadn't said what to do with the used pads, so I had a sack stuck back in my closet. I hated the sweet, metallic smell. I hated this creature I'd become.

WINTER settled in. Mother bought me heavy tights in three colors: navy, burgundy, brown. I took comfort in their texture and the snug, put-together sense they gave me, like my body before the blood. I even slept in them. That's how the blue ones got stained. When I was sure nobody was home, I washed them in cold water, then squeezed them out in a towel. But I felt ashamed to hang them in the bathroom. Of course I knew Daddy knew and, anyway, tights had to be washed in the normal order of things. But I couldn't do it. I draped them over the radiator in my room.

Mother didn't mention it. She didn't say it looked sloppy or that the drips would spot the floor. In a strange way I was on my own now, bound and free to make my own arrangements.

In the bottom of the Kotex box I found a folded order form:

*Send now for your copy:*

## WHAT EVERY GIRL SHOULD KNOW

Free pamphlet helps your daughter deal with the Facts and Fears of Growing Up

It showed a glowing mother and daughter holding the booklet between them. I looked at it and cried, like a child who's lost her mother in a department store. Where was that hand which would give me the pamphlet? Which would find me and take me home?

It never occurred to me to ask Daddy for information. Whatever this secret was, it was female. And all of a sudden that meant hidden and mute.

Now I wonder why I didn't send away for "What Every Girl Should Know" myself. Because Mother felt so strongly I shouldn't know it? Because I was afraid she'd see it when it came in the mail? That would be another exposure, lying flat on the kitchen table: pink and blond but still written in blood. Suddenly I was glad Drake was gone: he wouldn't have to know this. I'd be myself again before he got back.

Sure enough, on the fifteenth, the blood dried up. Saying I needed to check on Wig, who sometimes slept in the basement during the cold, I took my secret sack down, opened the iron furnace door, and set it in the flames. I could get ready for Drake now, for Christmas. Something of me was being cured, burned away.

# 15

WAITING IN THE train station for Drake, my heart danced the way it used to do for Santa Claus. He's on his way! Any minute! Any minute! Voices bounced hollow against the tile floor and walls, so my parents didn't talk much. We each waited for Drake, casting the nets of our attention out into the snowy night.

An hour after it was due, the train pulled in. Four hundred people got off in slow motion before Drake, wearing not only his uniform but a gray topcoat, appeared in the doorslot. He stepped down, and when his foot hit the pavement, I ran up and threw my arms around him.

"Merry Christmas!" I said, colliding with his shoulder.

"Welcome home, son." Daddy patted him on the back.

"My turn, Sumi," Mother declared, and her coat came between us.

"I have a box, too," Drake said, setting down his suitcase. "Excuse me."

He was in and out of the train in a moment. I offered to carry the box.

"Oh no you don't," he said, holding it out of my reach.

"Why not?"

His reply was to hum "White Christmas."

"Have you had dinner?" Mother asked.

"Oh yes, around Washington."

"Well, none of us could eat. We thought we'd stop at the Ideal on the way home."

The Ideal Café. Red-brown booths, each with a juke box selector, pages open like a Bible behind its glass dome. Home cooking: cornbread, pinto beans, catfish from the Holston.

We filed in, all separate, but soon the steam of overcooking and the smell of perpetual frying wilted the distance between us. Drake was laughing. I could tell he was nervous by the rattle in the middle of his laugh.

"Exams aren't till after vacation, you see, so some boys come back early. I don't want to do that, but I'll have to study at home. And practice."

"Don't they give you any break?" Mother sounded disappointed. "We always had exams before Christmas and then forgot about school till after the first of the year."

"School is one thing. But you can't forget about music," Drake told her.

"What a child!" she said, and Drake kicked me under the table.

Our thick plates came and we settled in to chopped greens and stewed tomatoes. Each coffee order came with a cream bottle tilted on the saucer. They reminded me of communion cups. "To home-coming!" I said, and Drake and I toasted. Neither of us like our coffee with cream.

THEY DON'T TEACH kids Humpty Dumpty for nothing. A thing goes and it's gone. You can pretend all you want out of need or fear, but you can't bring it back.

I thought about that as I put holly on the mantel. Until this year, Papa Gene had always brought us the holly, and mistletoe too, that he clipped from some tree he'd cut. This holly came from a florist. Its leaves were stiff, with points sharp as needles, its berries like big drops of blood. The whole family was different. Nothing would ever be easy again.

Drake wanted to know if I'd read the book he sent, which of course I hadn't.

"You can do it, Sumi," he said. "Don't let the style scare you."

"Why did you like it so much?" Drake was clipping fat lights onto the Christmas tree.

"I can't describe it. It's weird."

"How?"

"You'll have to read it."

"Okay," I promised. "Do you miss home?"

"Sure," he said, his head somewhere under branches. "I can't find the outlet."

"I can't see anything but your rear end and the tree."

"Wait, wait. I've got it." The tines hit the current and the blue spruce lit up. Color stood all over it like tears.

"Hey, Sumi, what's wrong?"

"I don't know. Papa Gene partly."

"Yeah, it's hard," Drake agreed. "Did you know he picked this tree? When I went to the sawmill yesterday, Chester said Papa Gene had his eye on this one for us since he worked that boundary in the spring."

"Does Mother know that?"

"I told her when I brought the tree home. You know what she said? 'That's Daddy. Still providing.' And it's true."

"Yes," I said. "I can see. It looks pretty, too, Drake. You've done a good job."

Drake always does a good job, slow and careful. Me, I've got the patience of a popcorn kernel in a hot pan.

"Drake—"

"What?"

I took a deep breath. "Do you like being away at school?"

He didn't hesitate. "It's the best thing that's ever happened to me. Mr. Johnson—he's my piano master—"

Master?

"—is extraordinary. He hears everything. Not just wrong notes, faulty phrasing, but what you don't play that you could. You know what he said to me about that Schumann?" He turned away from the tree to the piano. Leaning across the bench he played the opening, just a few notes, a figure, he would call it.

"What did he say?"

"I thought it was the best thing I did. You remember how I worked on it last summer. Anyway, Mr. Johnson listened, very coolly. Then he said, 'Technically it's excellent. Superb, really. And you imitate well.' "

"Imitate?" Drake never imitated anybody in his life. He even made up a way to walk.

"Yes. He told me which recording I'd listened to. 'You have it in your hands and your head,' he said, 'but you are not in *it*.' "

I thought about that. When Drake first began playing, he swayed a lot on the bench, leaning into the keys, his bright hair falling over his forehead.

"Sit still," Mother told him. "That's distracting." So he did. Was that what the piano master meant?

"So what do you do now?"

"Learn—no, find—another way to the music."

"How?"

"I'm not sure," Drake said, his hands turning to fists in his jeans pockets. "And my playing gets worse when I try. Even Wendy laughs."

I had already decided not to ask him about Wendy.

"That's rough. Does this guy know what he's doing?"

"Let's hope so." Drake smiled. "Anyway, I'm committed. How about *your* piano? How are lessons going?"

"Oh, Mrs. Conley's got me playing Bach."

"What Bach?"

"Two-Part Invention Number Fourteen," I told him.

Drake hummed the first phrase.

"Yep, that's it."

"And what about flute?"

"I can play a great rendition of 'Tulip Land.' "

He laughed. "Have to start somewhere. You ready for some lunch?"

"Sure."

"I'm done here. Mother said if I'd do the lights, she'd help us finish the tree tonight. But we've got to keep that cat of yours out of the ornaments."

Drake stacked boxes in the wing-backed chair while I picked up holly sprigs. Reaching for one under the magazine rack, I stepped on a clutch of berries. The red smear on the carpet jerked me out of our talk.

"I have to get something off the rug," I told Drake, and went to the kitchen to fetch the brush-bottle of upholstery cleaner.

As I knelt scrubbing, he said, "So how have you been?"

"Pretty good," I lied, working at the stain.

"You promised to write."

I can't tell you how hard I tried, I wanted to say, should have said, but my heart pushed at my throat. Finally I managed, "I don't really like sixth grade."

"Mrs. Scott, huh? She's not exactly the brightest lantern in the Cave."

I'd forgotten how Drake called our old maroon-halled school the Cave. This led to all sorts of jokes about which teachers were stalactites, which grades were Fat Man's Misery. What else had I forgotten?

"Just wait till next year," he went on. "The Lost River Cruise!" That's what he called the confusion when seventh graders change classes.

"Keezie moved," I told him, getting up. The stain was either gone or lost in the suds.

"You're kidding."

"Nope."

"Hey, that's terrible, Sumi. I'm sorry. I liked old Keezie. Where'd she go?"

"Williamson."

"Oh, I've been there," Drake said, "on a band trip. It's quite a place. They've got three elevators, not counting the ones at the hospital."

"Wow! Keezie'll love it."

"Yeah. There's nothing like an elevator to give you a lift."

So we laughed and ate pimento cheese and discussed what shopping we still needed to do. Christmas came and went like that; I never gave Drake the letters or talked about any real thing. I did give him a sweater, which he liked. His gift to me was a record. A strange-looking album with three people on the cover. Peter, Paul and Mary. They stood in front of a dirty brick wall with a heart chalked on it. She held flowers. How weird, I thought.

"Do you like this?" I asked Drake.

"Not especially. But Wendy does. It was her idea really. She thought—"

"Wendy!"

"What?"

"Wendy doesn't even—Oh, never mind. Thanks. I'll listen to it."

*But I won't*, I thought. *Besides, I don't even have a record player.*

"Listen to it on this," Drake said, disappearing

into the dining room, then the closet. He came back carrying the box he'd brought on the train. "My roommate has one of these, so I brought mine home for you."

"A body-building set!" I said. Drake made a face.

"Smarty!" he teased. It was his stereo.

"Wow! Oh thanks, Drake. Gee—"

"This is just a loan now. I'll want it back in the summer."

"Okay, if it hasn't taken root in my room."

"Things do," Mother said.

# 16

DRAKE WAS HOME till January third, and it snowed the whole time. On New Year's Eve, Mother and Daddy went to a party and Drake went to a movie, which left me alone. I didn't mind. Given the absence of Papa Gene and the presence of Wendy, we didn't seem together anyway.

If Granny Reeb was with us, everyone worried about her.

"How do you think she's bearing up?" Mother would ask Daddy in the kitchen. "Get Drake to play something cheerful."

When Granny Reeb wasn't there, it was Mother we looked to. Was she going to cry, staring at the chair where Papa Gene used to sit? Was she going to get angry? She didn't *do* these things, but she looked like she might. In fact, her only strange behavior was to go into the hall once and stand with her hands over her face.

When Daddy went to look for her, he said,

"Don't cry, Ivalea." From the living room I saw him put his arm around her shoulder, saw her back stiffen.

"I'm not crying," she said. "I'm witnessing."

When the door closed behind them on New Year's Eve, I decided to tour the house. I don't know why. I started in the basement, standing by the furnace, thinking of all it could burn, of the mountain of coal which had rolled down the stoker chute.

Up the stairs, I went into the kitchen, a big pine-paneled room with lots of windows. You couldn't tell it at night, but during the day it's as full of light as a pitcher is of cream. The sink, stove, and refrigerator are turquoise. Mother can't get over it. More than once she's said, "I don't know what the people who built this house were thinking of."

The kitchen has a door to the backyard, a little mowed space of mountain. Its other door goes into the dining room, crowded now with Granny Reeb's buffet. One end of the dark table is slanted where Daddy does bookkeeping. "I treat a variety of animals," he says, "but the billpayers are all mules."

Through the archway is the living room. It has a worn rug of roses, pink on a gray background. I've always loved that rug. When I was little I used to lie on my stomach and try to see *into* it, imagine the roses were clouds floating in a gray sky. I was floating too. And somewhere farther down than I could see was the earth, with this house on it, and in the house, a little girl, lying on the rug . . . It made me dizzy in a wonderful way just to think of it.

The living room is taken up mostly by Drake's grand piano. We got it second-hand (or hands) last year. There's also a fireplace, at the end opposite the dining room, and a rose-colored couch on the wall across from the front door. The Christmas tree. Chairs, too, and a hi-fi, its wooden lid half up like an oyster shell.

Daddy loves music as much as Drake. That's why he wanted us to learn piano. "All I can play," he used to say, "is the radio." But now he has this furniture that sings.

The front door leads out onto a big porch, green-floored, with a swing at one end. I stepped out for a few minutes and shivered, looking at the snowy yard and the waning moon.

Back in, I crossed to the little hall that leads to the half-bath and the stairs. I remember thinking as I went up how our house was a spiral, turning from the basement through the first floor to my room at the end of the curve. I was the youngest in the household, the last. It made sense where I was.

But when I got to my room, it didn't feel that way.

There was Daddy's college furniture painted

white, the green fern-patterned rug. My bed with Granny Reeb's coverlet which now has a flattened circle in the middle where Wig likes to sleep. I had the strangest feeling standing at my door—the feeling I'd had all fall looking in Drake's room—that the person who lived there was gone. Who was I then? A ghost? It gave me the creeps and I laughed to shake off the feeling. But the laugh didn't sound like me either.

Seizing on something to do to break the spell, I put on the record Drake had given me, then crawled around trying to plug the stereo in. Finally I got it.

I had many reasons not to like that record. I just put it on for the noise. Or maybe for back-handed spite: Okay, if it's somebody else's room, then I'll play somebody else's music.

Then came their voices:

> Well, early in the morning
> About the break of day
> I asked the Lord
> Help me find the way
> Help me find the way. . . .

It was very odd. Not at all like what I heard on the radio. Sort of like gospel, but the harmony was different. What kind of person was Wendy, if she liked this? Drake probably thought it was stupid.

Then came the second cut. It had a simple, lonely guitar sound and only the woman's voice:

> If you miss the train I'm on
> You will know that I am gone
> You can hear the whistle blow
> A hundred miles. . . .

In spite of myself I was drawn into the song. I'd grown up with train whistles, with heavy coal-loaded cars shaking the house.

> Lord I'm one, Lord I'm two
> Lord I'm three, Lord I'm four
> Lord I'm five hundred miles
> From my home. . . .

That's how I felt right there in my room, with everything familiar around me. Like I'd gone way off and could see our house, its windows streaming yellow light.

I started to cry. What had happened? I had been over every inch of the house and nothing had altered. Everything was just as it had been every New Year's Eve of my life. *It must be me*, I thought. *I don't belong. I've been cut loose, like the things in Drake's room when he left.* But it was more than that: losing Papa Gene and Keezie. Then the blood. All the changes.

Well, it was a new year now. A chance for me to choose some changes. I'd gotten a diary for Christmas and this seemed the time to start it. With my bathrobe on over my clothes, and Peter, Paul and Mary singing "Sorrow," I sat on the bed. The little gold key twirled at first, then caught in the lock. *Five Year Diary* was stenciled in gold on the green leatherette. I opened it to January first.

*Dear Diary,*

*Happy New Year! It's almost 1963 and I'm home alone. I'm twelve now and I'm going to make a new start. You'll see. Drake and Keezie are gone but you'll be my friend.*

*I'm short and plump, not tall and lanky like Drake, with no-color hair and blue eyes Daddy says he wished on me. Right now I'm sitting on my bed wearing the bathrobe Mother gave me for Christmas. It's got cherubs on it. Cherubs and candy. Baby stuff.*

*This page is supposed to hold five New Years, but I've already filled it. I'll have to write smaller.*

*Your friend as of tonight,*

*Sumi*

*(Stephanie Ann Mitchell)*

# 17

YOU CAN'T WRITE small enough. No matter how tight you hold the pen and squint your eyes, the words ruffle the line. I know, I tried. It's a step beyond writing letters you don't mail: writing things people can't read if they see them. It wasn't just in my diary; I wrote like that at school too. Even Mrs. Scott noticed.

"Are you in hot water, Sumi?" she asked.

"No. Why?"

"Your writing's shrunk something awful. Going to have to get a magnifying glass to read it."

"Sorry," I said, and tried to let in more space. But it was hard. Anything could happen if you opened up those letters. The emptiest wind in the world could blow right through.

AFTER ALL that snow at Christmas, January played at spring. It made Daddy nervous. "We'll be shoveling through the drifts next month, you'll see.

And when the rains come in March . . . I don't like it. Not one bit."

He was worried about floods.

We were all worried about Granny Reeb going to Akron on the bus, but she refused to be driven. "I'll be fine by myself," she insisted. "Besides, I'd be worried sick about Ivalea driving back."

Granny Reeb was going to spend the winter with Uncle Hal and his family.

"A change will do you good," Mother had told her.

Granny Reeb smiled a tight smile. "Not if it's like the changes I've had lately."

But she went. We saw her off on a Saturday morning so mild it could have been April.

The temporary spring helped things at school. At recess and lunchtime we didn't have to choose between huddling in the Cave and shivering on the playground. We could run again. That was strange, too. Something about winter remembering early fall made the sixth graders act like little kids. We played games. Together. All that year the boys had played some form of sports while the girls stood around trying to look like somebody else. But the thaw saw us in two lines across the gravel, chanting Red Rover.

My team boasted Ollie Traynor but the other side had Angie Sizemore. They were the Atlases of the sixth grade. Angie was beautiful, too.

We dared Cathy Blanchard and Dale Rowlett and Jimmy Steele. Only Jimmy broke through, hurling himself at the line of arms like a rocket aimed for outer space. Then it was the other side's turn.

"Red Rover, Red Rover,
We dare Sumi over!"

I was surprised to be called first. The line swayed so I couldn't gauge the position of locked hands.

"You can do it, Sumi!" Ollie called.

Sure I could. I'd won the neighborhood contest for hanging longest upside down. The P. E. teacher used to say I flew down the basketball court. I took my place about four feet behind our line.

"Red Rover, Red Rover—"

They were calling louder now. I wound myself up inside like a spring. I charged like a bull.

My aim was the link between Rose Fletcher and Jan Lewis. Both were professionally weak, always holding one arm out with its hand dangling like a broken paw.

"Red Rover, Red—"

"Go, Sumi!"

But right before I got there the whole line shifted

to the left and it was the Saylor twins' hands I slammed into. They caught my diaphragm just right and I lost my lunch.

At first there were hoots of laughter. Then kids in clumps moved away. Ollie called Mrs. Waltz, who was on playground duty.

"My goodness, Sumi," she said, coming up behind me, leaning over to put her hands on my shoulders.

"I'm okay," I said, trying not to let her see I was crying. I was humiliated as much as hurt. She gave me a Kleenex from her purse.

"Here. Stand up. Let's get you to the rest room."

On the corner, somebody began ringing the bell and kids swarmed in. Mrs. Waltz and I stood waiting. I was mortified that she'd seen the patch of vomit at my feet.

"I'll send someone to clean it up. Were you sick before the game, honey?" She smoothed my hair back, like I was the little girl who had sat in her third-grade class.

That, combined with her calling me "honey," loosened a catch in my throat. Tears and words poured out.

"It wasn't fair. They switched. I could have done it. Ask Ollie. He saw—"

She listened, one arm around my shoulder, guiding me into the building.

"You're all right, Sumi. It'll be all right."

She took me into the cold, smelly bathroom, cleared paper towels clogging one sink, and let the water run hot. At the other sink she dampened a paper towel with cool water.

"Hold this on your forehead," she told me.

From her purse she took a washcloth, held it under the hot water, squeezed it out, and then sponged my face and hands.

"Thank you. I'm okay now."

"Not quite. You've skinned your knee too." Squatting down, she dabbed at my knee. "Now I want you to go to the office and lie down."

"But—"

"No *buts*, Sumi. Just for half an hour, to make sure your stomach's all right. I'll tell Mrs. Scott."

"Well, thank you."

We pushed through the swinging door into the hall. It was dark but at least it smelled better.

"Can you make it upstairs by yourself?"

"Sure."

"Well, tell Miss Combs I sent you and said she should keep you till one o'clock."

"Yes ma'am."

Mrs. Waltz went down the hall to her room and I headed for the stairs. There was no reason she should walk with me, but I found myself shivering because she was gone.

# 18

IN SOCIAL STUDIES last year we learned about the Continental Divide. It runs along the top of mountains; all the rivers on one side flow east and all flow west on the other. That's what the Red Rover day was for me. Not a turning point. A line to cross. And everything from then on went in a different direction.

I walked to the office and lay down, then in a half hour went back to class. I thought they would all stare at me, the girl who threw up on the playground. But nobody noticed.

Next day Mrs. Waltz stopped me in the hall. "Got your breath back, Sumi?"

"Oh sure," I said.

"No gravel rooted in your knee?"

I shook my head.

"Good." She smiled and went on.

Her smile made me smile back, and smiling felt

sweet and funny, like bare arms after a winter of sleeves. I began to think about Mrs. Waltz.

She had the brightest classroom in the building. All the other walls were institution green; she managed to have hers painted yellow and pale blue. When Keezie and I were in her third grade, she took an interest in us. We wanted to send a rocket to the moon and she helped us write the president about it. We thought it would be only fair to let him know.

Since there was no elementary library, Mrs. Waltz brought in books for us to read and introduced us to mail-order book clubs. Keezie and I were her biggest customers. The day those book boxes came I was ecstatic. I'd sit and smell each book, run the smooth cover over my cheek. This was mine, every page of it!

And Mrs. Waltz loved parties. Along with homeroom mothers, she provided us with not just the usual Halloween, Christmas, and Valentine's treats, but celebrations for Thanksgiving, St. Patrick's Day, Easter, and the first of May. She had a whole storeful of decorations in that little supply closet: witches to leprechauns to bunnies, even mermaids!

She was pretty too. Small-boned with curly brown hair and blue-green eyes. And she loved clothes. Everything she wore was interesting. Her loafers might be red, her skirt green with blue inside the pleats. I was fascinated.

Not so much in third grade as in sixth. Scrambling around for clues of how to be, I latched onto Mrs. Waltz. The more I watched, the more I wanted to be just like her: light and laughing, sure of what to do. Maybe if I talked to her—

My heart jumped every time I thought about it. How would it be? What would I say to her? She'd be standing by the silver radiators at recess, drinking a Coke. I'd have on my best clothes, a cherry red skirt and sweater made of something called Cashemiracle. "Mrs. Waltz," I'd begin . . .

But what? What was it I wanted to say? To ask? I didn't know.

My solution for the time being was to avoid her, stepping carefully like I carried a thing that might spill.

BUT SOMETHING else spilled near the end of January, a truth I hadn't guessed. Snow had come again, over ankles, halfway up the tires of the cars. Mother came in to tell me school was closed. I sat up in bed, woozy.

"Just rest awhile," she said. So I did.

When light woke me an hour or so later, I still didn't feel right. A spiral in the middle of me clenched and hurt and let go. I climbed out of bed and was reaching for my robe when I felt it. I knew it was blood, though I had no idea why. I went shaking to the bathroom, then realized I would need the supplies in my closet. This couldn't be happening.

Daddy had gone on to work, but Mother was in the kitchen scraping carrots.

"Good morning," I ventured.

"Hey, sleepyhead," she said over her shoulder. "I'm making us a big pot of vegetable soup."

"Mother—"

"What, Sumi? Have some coffee. It's fresh."

"It's just—" I stood there, mortified. She turned around. "There's more blood."

"Well, of course, Sumi. I thought you understood."

"Understood what?" I bit my lip.

"That you're going to have . . ." she hesitated, "these *times* every month now."

I tried to control my horrified face.

"Grown-up women do," she said. "You'll get used to it."

# 19

I THINK that's part of my trouble: I don't get used to things. I still expect Drake to wake me in the night, calling "Stee-rike two!" I'll sit up in bed, look through our open doors and see him, sitting up too, sound asleep, calling a Reds game. And when we set out for Granny Reeb's, I think it's her *house* we're going to, expect to watch through the door-glass as she comes from the kitchen, wiping her hands on a towel. Papa Gene's just at work. He'd never die and leave her.

I did quit looking for Keezie at school, I'll say that. I talked to her in my head some, the way I used to write to Drake. But I had lost my voice as far as letters were concerned, just wrote a little in my diary. I'd only had a postcard from Keezie any-way. "Second trumpet!" it said. I'd sent a Christmas card, but what can you say on a card? I didn't want to tell her I was still splitting octaves on the flute. In my mind I asked what she knew about the bleeding, why it happens, what we're supposed to do. And she said it has to do with a curse on Eve. All this for one apple? I asked her. She didn't think it was funny either.

*Mrs. Waltz has to know*, I thought. *She must go through it, too*. But there was no way I could bring it up. I didn't have the words.

Still there had to be something I could say to her. I began going in at recess to try. There'd be her own kids waiting to talk and, by the time they'd finished, I'd have memorized what was on her desk and forgotten what I had planned to say.

"Hello, Sumi," she'd begin. "What a neat sweater!"

"Thanks," I'd answer, even that word hard to get off my tongue.

"How's sixth grade treating you?"

"Fine."

"Do you think this weather will ever—?" But then another child would run in or the electric bell would drill its hole in the air. "Guess I'd better get back to work," she'd say.

I began to hunt different things to wear. Her clothes were so happy. And I began to wish even more that I wasn't plump. Clothes didn't look as good and boys wouldn't like me. Right then there weren't any boys I cared about, but I knew I had to start thinking. It came with the territory.

Mother liked my interest in clothes and losing

weight. "Dieting won't hurt you if we do it sensibly," she told me. That meant skim milk and healthy cereal or a poached egg for breakfast; lean meat, cottage cheese, and some naked vegetable for dinner. "At lunch you'll just have to do the best you can."

I decided the best would be not to eat at all. And, if I spent the lunch hour walking, I'd be killing two birds with one stone.

Of course Mother still gave me lunch money. I kept it in a jar in my dresser drawer.

Mrs. Waltz went home for lunch. I knew where her house was. I knew her car, too. She'd driven that blue Buick when Keezie and I were her kids.

That's what she calls every classful. "My kids are special," she says. And they do seem to brighten up in her room. The snowflakes taped on her windows are always the best in the school.

February came and I knew what to do with the lunch money: I'd get her a valentine! Just to say thanks for having been my teacher and for almost, even now, being my friend. But what would be the right thing?

Daddy always got Mother perfume and me a heart-box of candy. Mrs. Waltz liked candy. She'd told us once she had to choose between a Coke and a candy bar at recess. "I could live on sugar," she'd said, "if I wouldn't outgrow my clothes." So that would be it.

A few blocks from school was a drugstore. Some kids went there for lunch, so it wasn't odd for me to turn up. I looked at the display of hearts inside the glass case. There were great big ones topped with roses like floppy hats. That wouldn't do. I wanted something simple but beautiful too, like the heart drawn on the wall on the Peter, Paul and Mary album.

For several days I went every lunch hour and looked. Hamburgers sizzling on the grill made me hungry and sick. Finally I chose the next-to-smallest heart, white, with a red rose. I figured it had maybe nine pieces in it. That was good. I was in the sixth grade and she taught the third grade and if you put that together, well--6 + 3 = 9.

But how could I give it to her?

I couldn't. I'd leave it on her desk. With a note? I puzzled over that. I wanted her to know who it was from but I couldn't think of what to say.

When the day came I got to school early. Mrs. Waltz's door was open but the room was empty. I walked into that huge space—no giggles yet, no chalk dust—slipped the heart out of my coat and laid it in the center of the desk. I was out in the hall by the water fountain before my own heart settled down.

Not knowing what to say, I didn't look for her at lunch or afternoon recess. Then came our class party. True to form, Mrs. Scott had had us make our own valentine boxes and then had given a prize for the best. Cathy won—hers looked like a wedding cake festooned with blood—and I came in second. But when we opened our glorified shoeboxes, Cathy's was full and mine only had five cards, one of which I'd put in myself. On the back of the puppy who said "Doggone! Be my valentine!" I had penciled with my left hand:

# Your Secret Pal

I took care to change the way I made my *e*'s. Drake says *e*'s are dead giveaways, even if you write wronghanded.

Nobody looked at my valentines of course. They were too busy going through their own wads. Only Mrs. Scott saw when she came back to give me second prize, a Goo-Goo candy cluster. Just what I needed. The other girls were leaning over each other's shoulders, purring and exclaiming, and the boys were drinking RC's and kicking box tops and ribbons that had fallen to the floor.

Suddenly Rose flashed her cute smile at me. "How many valentines did you get, Sumi?"

"Five."

"Oh."

"One of them wasn't signed."

"Well," she said, "it doesn't really matter how many you get. You won the prize!"

"Yes," I agreed. I could pretend if she could. But I thought the party would never be over.

When it was, I made short work of gathering my stuff and getting out. I was headed down the hall full speed when I ran into Mrs. Waltz.

"Sumi," she said, "I was hoping to see you. Do you know anything about a box of valentine candy that turned up on my desk?"

I know it's white, I thought. I know it cost $2.95, all in change.

"No," I said.

"Are you sure, Sumi?" She looked worried.

"Well, yes. I mean no. It's for you. I thought you liked candy."

"I do," she said, struggling to put a smile on top of everything else in her face. "And it's sweet of you, Sumi. But you shouldn't spend your money on me."

"That's okay," I said. Why was *she* embarrassed?

"But thank you very much. Look, do you want a ride home? You've got an awful lot to carry."

"No, I can make it." Even as I heard the words, I wished I could take them back.

"See you tomorrow, then," she said. "Happy Valentine's!"

"You, too," I answered.

Mrs. Waltz had delayed me. Cathy and a procession of girls were starting down the hall.

"Hey, Sumi!" Cathy called.

I looked at her, buttoned slimly in a green loden coat, with a white tam perfect against her hair. She looked like an ad in *American Girl*. She must have gotten valentines from everybody—I'd seen the stack in her hand. And then she'd won the first prize, too.

"Gotta run!" I yelled and took the stairs three at a time.

My arms were too full for me to navigate Death Valley, but I wanted to avoid Cathy and company along the highway, so I chose a middle path. It took me through the poorest part of Talmidge, where houses were shored up with RC Cola signs and frozen laundry fought the wind. Tears burned my cheeks.

When I checked the mailbox at home, I found a postcard from Drake. It had an old picture of his school on the front, and on the back, in red ink, *Happy Hearts!*

# 20

I REALLY can't tell what happened next. Oh, I know the facts, and I could put them down in a column and rearrange them till I get the right order, but they would never add up to what happened. Maybe life is more like chemistry than math: put two events together and the result is not their sum but a new substance altogether.

I kept trying to talk to Mrs. Waltz and it kept not working. I couldn't find words. If she had any idea something was wrong, she didn't show it, though once she came back early from lunch so we could talk. It had taken me two weeks to get up the courage to ask her and then, standing in that steamy room, I couldn't meet her eyes, looked instead at the March sky caged in the window. All that I couldn't say stood like a wall between us; all that I didn't understand swelled in me till I thought my ribs would crack. "I love you" was the only message I could think of, and I couldn't say *that*. It didn't make any sense.

I tried to write to Keezie about it.

*Dear Keezie,*

*Remember Mrs. Waltz, our third grade teacher? How she always listened? Well, I've been missing you a lot, and I thought maybe I could talk to her the way we used to, the way we talked, but Keezie, something happens every time I try. It's like I go dumb. Do you think there could be something wrong with the air in her room?*

But I couldn't joke about it. What was wrong was me. This was what was so scary. Something was the matter with me.

The obvious thing to work on was how I looked. I spent hours following the curler diagrams in *Seventeen*, but my hair just parted where the curlers had been, the way a church is divided into aisles.

I washed my face with special soap Mother bought, but it stayed broken out. And pimples didn't look incidental on me, the way they did on most kids. They looked like they belonged there.

I studied my face in the mirror. No clear outline, no clean features. I put makeup on to try to give it some focus, but makeup just made the blur shine.

It was like my overall shape. I had a waist but it

was too big and too high, so my beginning breasts looked like flab. Granny Reeb had given me a training bra for Christmas. Expando-Cup, it said. But I didn't really want to expand. There was too much of me already.

You could tell by my clothes. On the hangers they looked perfect, but on me they pinched or stuck out or drooped, collars too big, sleeves cutting under the arms.

At night I'd roll my hair and choose my clothes, hoping for a transformation by morning. *Total make-over*, the magazines promised. *Find a new you!* But it was always the old me that Daddy woke up. A click, then light, then the smell of Lectric Shave, and finally Daddy's voice.

"You awake in there, Sumi?"

"Un-huh," I'd mutter. On the bed Wig stretched and kneaded and yawned.

"What's $25 \times 35$?"

"I have no idea."

"Well, figure it out while I go find a tie."

And I'd lie there, head dented by brush rollers, trying to find the multiplication tables in my brain. Where Daddy got the idea of waking us like that, I don't know, but Drake says he's been doing it forever.

I'd still be trying to yank out the dreams and haul in the numbers when he'd reappear.

"Well? What's 25 × 35?"

"Is it 625?" I'd ask. I knew that was the answer to something.

"Sumi, 625? Now, honey, you know that 25 × 25 is 625. Are you awake?"

"I think so."

"Then get on up now. I've got to get to work."

" 'Bye, Daddy."

And I would get up, wash, take down my hair, then stretch and pull my way into the outfit I'd laid out. Once again, the girl who should have been there didn't show up. I had to make myself go downstairs and face breakfast.

"Reproached egg," Mother called it. She didn't eat eggs at all and sympathized when I shivered back at the one that shook on my plate. But I ate it, along with every bite of diet toast. It was a long time till dinner.

All through breakfast I could feel the weight of school lean toward me. But there was no place else to go.

I decided to experiment. One week I avoided Mrs. Waltz, ducking into the bathroom or another class if she came down the hall, crossing the street if I saw her headed for the playground. It was miserable.

Another week I gave up answering in class. I kept my hands to my side and, if Mrs. Scott called on me, I just said I didn't know. It worked for Cathy—

why not me? But by Wednesday Jan said I was showing off.

"You *know* she knows, Mrs. Scott." (Jan always says Miz-riz, like being married and misery are close kin.)

"Yeah, come on Sumi," Dale Rowlett coaxed. "Give us the answer."

I held out another day, but then Mrs. Scott stopped me after school.

"I think Jan's right, Sumi," she told me. "I think you do know the answers. What's going on?"

What could I say? Could I tell her that I'd tried not reading the assignments just so I wouldn't know? And that I hated that too?

"I just get tired of being the one to answer is all."

"Well, that's some complaint! There's many a child who would thank their lucky stars to have such a problem! You're smart as a whip, you and your brother both, and that's a *responsiblility*, Sumi. Don't let yourself down."

"Yes ma'am."

"It's so *easy* for you. You just don't realize—"

*You don't realize either*, I thought. *You don't even know what this is about.* But I said, "I'll do better."

"Okay. See that you do. I wouldn't want to have to call your parents."

"Oh, no." I hadn't thought of that. I could never explain to Daddy. He was so proud.

So I went back to knowing what I knew. I'd have

to be smart as well as fat and plain. But how did Cathy get away with pretending? She knew as much as I did. All her homework papers and tests were A's. Yet somehow she managed to hide in the classroom, always sweetly, beautifully, declining to know. But then, clothes fit her, too. Her hair had its own style and she didn't need makeup. Her skin was clear and creamy, except when the least attention pinkened her cheeks. It worked like a charm when she denied ever having heard of Sarajevo, when she said in smooth music she had no idea who we fought with in The Great War.

# 21

EASTER CAME in late March. I had hoped Drake would come home but he had to be in a piano competition. So it was just the three of us.

The Saturday before, Mother took me out to get a dress. We started with size thirteens, choosing a black one with tuxedo-white bib and cuffs. It hung on me.

"Why, Sumi, I had no idea you'd lost this much. Look at her, Lynn." She motioned for the clerk. "Sumi's really slimming down."

"Law, yes," she said happily. "Let me hunt that in a smaller size."

They didn't have it, though. I wound up taking a knit suit, robin's-egg blue, with white buttons like stubs of chalk.

Mother and I celebrated by having a cottage cheese lunch at the drugstore. I couldn't eat all of mine.

"You don't want to overdo it and lose too fast

now, Sumi. Don't forget you have to have protein."

"I know," I assured her. "I'm just full." It was partly excitement and partly the fact that I wasn't used to eating lunch.

"Let's go then. I have to get your father a shirt at Collier's before we go home."

Daddy's church days are limited to Christmas and Easter, and he always requires a fresh shirt. The other Sundays—his only day off—he takes his worship in the bath while we're holding hymnals. Like Emily Dickinson:

Some keep the Sabbath going to church
I keep it staying at home. . . .

He quoted that to Mother the one time she said she wished he'd come with us.

That night when I modeled my suit, Daddy too had praise. "It looks great, Sumi. I wish I had your willpower." He patted his stomach. "If it weren't for biscuits and gravy I'd do all right."

"We don't *have* to have biscuits and gravy," Mother reminded him.

"Now that's where we differ. Maybe you women can get by on bone juice and crackers, but a man has to have something to stick to his ribs."

She smiled. "Well, you've got it."

Daddy laughed. "But Sumi here knows what's

good for her. Do you need new shoes to go with that?"

It turned out I did. And do you know they had to be smaller too? I never knew you could lose weight in your feet. I didn't even know mine were fat.

I didn't know a lot of things. Like the fact that once I started losing weight it would be hard to stop.

WHEN KIDS at school began noticing, I was thrilled.

"Wish I could lose weight and get new clothes," Rose Fletcher said, braiding and unbraiding the tail of her long blond hair. "But I don't have any weight to lose."

I still felt like I did. In addition to my lunchtime walks, I started doing exercises in my room at night. I'd put on my Peter, Paul and Mary album—the fast songs worked best—and bend and stretch and bicycle till my ears rang. I especially liked "If I Had My Way," about Samson tearing down his prison. I loved the sound of the guitar and I loved the words. I was tearing down something, too, or getting free of it, like it said in the song we sang at church:

> This house of flesh
> Is but a prison.

Bars of bone
They hold my soul. . . .

I felt like I'd been held long enough.

MRS. SCOTT teased, "You keep this up and you'll be no bigger than a minute."

But Mrs. Waltz said nothing. Maybe my silent presence had started to get on her nerves. She would notice if I lost more, though. She would have to.

Then April Fool's Day I woke up and couldn't eat. Mother said I'd seen one reproached egg too many, so she'd get some high-powered cereal on the way home. Next morning I couldn't eat that either. Dinner had gone down okay but I knew if I ate one flake I'd be sick.

"Are you regular?" Mother asked.

"Sure."

"Monthlies too?"

"No problem."

"It's probably a virus then. Why don't you go back to bed?"

"I'm not sick, honest. And we're having try-outs for promotion in band." We were but that didn't matter to me. My flute-playing was pitiful. The truth was Mrs. Waltz had hall duty that week.

"All right, but be sure you eat a good lunch."

I nodded. Was a nod a lie?

"Sumi—" she brushed her hand across my hair. It made me want to cry. "Well, come on then. We don't want to be late."

I WAS still able to eat some dinner, though it felt like food got bigger when I put it in my mouth. Breakfast I managed by coming down late and pretending to eat while Mother fixed her hair. I could put the cereal down the disposal when I rinsed my bowl.

Then one night, past the middle of April—I know because the talk of taxes had died down—I took one bite of stuffed pork chop and ran to the bathroom and threw up.

Panic hit as soon as the heaving stopped. I couldn't get away with this. They'd make me eat or go to the doctor and I couldn't do either.

Mother thought my tears were from being sick. She wet a washcloth and blotted my face.

"Now go lie down and I'll bring you some Coke in a minute."

So I did. I turned on Peter, Paul and Mary and stretched out on my bed, feeling thin as the coverlet itself, feeling light as the little wind that made the shutter hinge sing. My thoughts seemed to leave my head and drift away on guitar notes. The rhythm was about to put me to sleep when Mother opened the door.

"Sumi," she began, "has anyone at school had mono?"

"Not that I know of." There was a pause while she plumped pillows and slid them behind my back. When I was sitting up and stable, she handed me the Coke.

"Well, I think I would have heard about it. But I feel sure you've got some kind of infection. You're losing weight too fast and your color's not good. I'm going to call Dr. Goss tomorrow."

"No! I mean, I'm okay, really. I'll bet I could eat some applesauce right now." She had made cinnamon applesauce to go with the pork.

"Let me get you some then."

I sipped Coke and reasoned with my stomach while she was gone. It was only applesauce. It wouldn't make me *that* fat. And it was mild, easy to swallow.

But it wasn't. On my tongue it seemed to swell up, like gelatin sprinkled on water. I brought the spoon back out. "Maybe later."

"That settles it. I'll call him in the morning." She rearranged the pillows again, checked my forehead for fever. "You try to get some rest."

Strangely enough, worried as I was, I fell right asleep. And all night long I dreamed about Drake. We were in an old house with high ceilings and dark heavy doors which slid into the walls. Drake had found it while riding his bike and had come home to get me.

Buttresses of dusty light slanted through every room. We walked and talked quietly, as though in a museum. Then suddenly Drake leapt ahead and slid the great doors between us. "Bet you can't catch me!" he taunted. And the chase was on.

I wasn't scared. Drake's bigger but I'm faster, and he didn't know his way around this territory any better than I did. Those doors were heavy, though. By the time I slid them back enough to slip through, Drake was gone from the next room. I could hear him off to the left, so I dashed down the hall.

Even for a dream-hall it was strange, curving and leading down. It made me dizzy as I ran, but I also felt exhilarated until I heard Drake's laugh crack behind me.

I wheeled around to see not the hall I'd been following, but the base of a huge staircase, carved, rising maybe thirty steps to a landing, then turning into two staircases which rose perpendicular to that.

"Drake!" I yelled. And he answered. Not by voice but by some motion, like a bird's shadow. I flew up the staircase, turned right, and then right again as the flight of stairs doubled back. I could see no end to them, rising and angling, changing from carved walnut to varnished pine to metal and then to only a roughing-in where steps were to be built. But I kept running. I was breathing so hard the air bounced off my lungs like a ball. I couldn't see Drake, I couldn't hear him, but I knew he was there somewhere. I had to keep going.

Just as I hit the last flight, the one whose steps were anchored on air, the alarm clock rang in my parents' room and I jerked awake. It was six-thirty, I knew. Too early for me to get up, but my heart was making too much racket for me to sleep.

# 22

I TURNED on my bedside lamp and reached under the bed for the book Drake had sent. Maybe if I looked for him where he said he'd been . . .

But the words were no more connected for me than that last skeletal staircase. I couldn't climb any higher. Drake wasn't there anyway. I was suddenly sure of it. What I'd thought was his answer was my own shadow, or the curve of my hair shading my face. Drake was gone.

At the back of my throat something caught like a hook. When it let go, there came enough tears to soak a feather pillow. I felt like my elbows cried and my ankles; my toes bent back, my collarbone ached. I felt empty and full like a shell scoured by the sea.

Then Daddy snapped on the overhead light.

"Good morning, Glory! What's 45 × 15?"

"More than it should be."

He laughed. "You must not be too bad off. Your

mother says go ahead and get up even though you're not going to school. Dr. Goss might be able to work you in first thing."

"Okay, Daddy."

"And Sumi—"

"Yes?"

"That's an easy one. You know 10 × 45 is 450 and half that again is 225, so the answer is 675. See? You don't even have to multiply out."

"I see." Did he *dream* about this stuff?

"Always good to have a short cut."

"Um-hmm," I said.

"Call me about the doctor."

"Yes, Daddy."

I sat up in bed, light-headed from all that crying, and opened the shutter. Down on the ground the daffodils were leaning with the wind. I waved at them. I felt that new.

DR. GOSS'S nurse, Mrs. Carson, snapped her wrist and whipped the air with her starched cuff. How could the mercury ever rise in thermometers she shook down?

"Your girl does look peaked," she told my mother. "Open up there."

I fought not to gag.

Staring at her watch, Mrs. Carson went on. "Not eating well. How much weight has she lost?"

"Fifteen pounds, I think."

Twenty. I was glad I couldn't open my mouth.

"Since when?"

"The first of the year."

"That's too much. Could she have worms?"

"Worms!" Mother sat up as though she'd been slapped. "Surely not."

Mrs. Carson went on. "Kids get them at school. We see a fair amount here."

"Well, check then, of course," Mother told her. "But I'd be more than surprised—"

"Time's up." She retrieved the thermometer and brought it to exactly the place where her watch had been, as though that were the only spot where she could see. "Normal," she pronounced. "You get your clothes off."

I liked her toughness. Bobby pins sutured her twist of gray hair like a wound.

A corner of the room was taken up with a metal screen to undress behind. It was cold, as was the steel-topped table beside it, and the white metal chair which held my things. I put on what felt like a tablecloth and came out.

We waited and waited. I started to shiver. Finally the door opened but it was only Mrs. Carson. "Forgot to get a weight on you," she said. "He'll want that."

So I followed her out to the hall. I tried to wish myself heavy, the wolf in Red Riding Hood filled with stones. I remembered when I used to watch

Mrs. Carson nudge that scale-weight and hope it wouldn't go past twenty. This day I prayed it would balance past five. It didn't.

"One hundred and four," she told the hall, then inked it onto the chart. "Get back in there before you freeze."

Mother had her head in her hands.

"Are you all right?" I asked.

"Just a little sleepy," she said. "Waiting for doctors wears me out. How much do you weigh?"

"A hundred and four."

"Ummm."

The lock clicked and Dr. Goss came in behind me.

"Well, Miss Mitchell," he said, resting his big warm hands on my shoulders, "looks like you've got a problem people would kill for."

I smiled. Mother stood up. "Hello, Dr. Goss. How are you?"

"Except for flu, low blood, chicken pox, and premature labor, I'm doing fine," he told her. "And yourself?"

"Well enough." She shook his hand. Mother isn't short, but Dr. Goss had to lean to bring his face nearer hers.

"Sorry about your daddy."

"Thank you."

"A good man." He studied my chart. "Let me see. Sumi, you sit right up here." He patted the examination table. "Mrs. Mitchell, I believe I'd do well to see Sumi by herself for a few minutes, if you don't mind. Just ask Mrs. Carson to step back in as you leave."

"All right," she said. I hadn't expected this.

He listened to my heart, the stethoscope like a cold mouth on my chest.

"That'll last," he told me. Then he thumped on my back and listened there. "Deep breath," he instructed. "Now let it out. Umm. Quite a rib cage."

He had me lie on my back. "Is that sore?" he asked, rolling his cupped hand on my abdomen.

"A little."

"Sit up."

With his lighted funnel, he checked eyes and ears, looked down the cave of my throat. Then he stood back, arms folded. His thick gray hair seemed to weight his head forward and bristly eyebrows threatened to close his eyes.

"Tell me what you eat."

I listed the menu we had planned for breakfast and dinner.

"From what I hear you haven't been eating much of that." He fiddled with things in his pocket. "What about lunch?"

I had already decided to say chicken soup, crackers, and milk, all of which you could get at the drugstore.

"I skip lunch," I told him.

"Does your mother know this?"

I shook my head. The rest of me started shaking. He turned to Mrs. Carson. "Did Mrs. Mitchell say whether she'd started menstruating yet?"

"No. Have you?"

They both looked at me.

"Started your periods?" she went on.

I didn't know what she was talking about.

"Evidently not," she told him. Then it dawned on me what she meant.

"Oh. Mother never used those words," I said. "I've been bleeding since December."

"All the time?" Dr. Goss's eyebrows were up.

"No, you know, just monthly."

"Has losing weight affected that?"

"No."

"Well, if you keep this up, it will."

That sounded like a warning.

"And you know what that means, Sumi?" He rolled the examination stool over and sat down in front of me. Again I shook my head.

"It means when you're grown up, you might not be able to have babies."

"Babies!"

He nodded.

"You mean because you have to gain weight to have a baby?"

He studied me for a minute, parting his moustache with his thumb and forefinger.

"No. I mean if you don't eat right and you lose too much weight, your periods will stop altogether, because your body will quit releasing eggs."

"Eggs?"

He looked at Mrs. Carson, who gave him the slightest nod.

"Sumi, what did your mother tell you about menstruation?"

*She didn't tell me that terrible word*, I thought. "Nothing, except I was growing up and it would happen once a month."

"Ah! And has it been painful?"

"Not much."

"Sometimes it is at first. Your body's getting ready so when *you're* ready, you'll be able to conceive and bear a child."

Heat went all over me, as if I stood in front of a fire. I hugged myself. "Really?"

"Absolutely," he said.

All this had to do with babies? I felt glad, relieved somehow. At least there was a reason. Why hadn't Mother told me? I wrapped myself tighter in my arms.

"So you have to be careful. You have to remember your body can do something besides wear clothes."

"Yes," I said. And I saw my body leaping those dream-stairs after Drake; I saw my leg swing over the branch that was the first step up my favorite tree. I had barely moved since December.

This body I'd been starving used to race the sunset down Third Street, used to knock a softball over Mrs. Henley's wash, then fly through the diamond home. This was my body. If I ever had children, I'd be running relay races with them. If I didn't, I'd be learning to snow-ski, I'd be floating smack in the middle of the lake in the sun.

"So what do you say?" Dr. Goss asked.

Hadn't I answered? Had I just sat there glowing?

"I'm hungry," I said.

# 23

I SAT in the waiting room while Mother talked with Dr. Goss. It was crowded, as always. Feverish children kept sliding off laps; old people were so sick or tired they leaned their heads against the walls.

Mrs. Carson was not only the nurse but the receptionist and bookkeeper as well. In a few minutes Mother came out the door and crossed over to the payment window. When she finished with Mrs. Carson, she turned, collecting me with her look.

I was scared. What had Dr. Goss told her? What would she say? At the same time I felt, as we walked to the car, something new that the fear couldn't touch.

When the engine caught, Mother took a deep breath. "Dr. Goss wants to do some tests, Sumi. I'll run you by the lab this afternoon. But he doesn't expect to find anything. He thinks it's just that we've been overdoing it, the diet business, I mean.

He says girls your age have to be careful losing weight with so much growing going on."

"So what should we do?" I asked. The *we* felt funny, but Mother had said it and I didn't want to leave her out.

"See that you eat regular meals and get enough exercise."

"But won't I gain weight?"

"Probably not, if you avoid desserts and potato chips, things that aren't good for you anyway. And it wouldn't hurt to gain a little—"

I didn't intend to, though. "Okay," I said.

"That means no more skipping lunch," she warned.

"Yes ma'am." I waited for her to get mad but she didn't. I waited while we drove past the drugstore, the gas station . . .

"Mother?"

"Yes?" She kept her eyes on the narrow road, cut between mountain and river.

"Dr. Goss told me . . ." For a minute I was stuck. "He told me that having periods means you can have babies."

"Well, of course."

"You didn't tell me that."

"You're not old enough."

"But I'm old enough to—"

"Let me finish." She snapped the turn signal. We were almost home now. "You're not old enough to know about certain things and all the worry that comes with them."

"But Mother—"

"Sumi, this is for me to decide. You're only twelve." She pulled us neatly into the drive. "You've got years to think about such things. Enjoy your childhood while it lasts."

But it's *over*, I wanted to tell her. Can't you see? You can't say "Hatch later," and push me back in the egg. But there was no point in it. Here we were. She was getting out of the car.

THAT NIGHT I ate Jell-O and soup. The next morning I packed a lunch, since everything the cafeteria dished up weighed a ton. And I had to find someone to sit with. At first I tried Ann Jones and Libby Miller, the girls I used to stand with on the playground. But soon I realized they were friends now and didn't want anybody else.

So one day I just plopped down beside Cathy. "Do you really not know where Venezuela is?" I asked her.

"Venezuela! We haven't had that since last fall!"

"You do, don't you?"

She just smiled. "I like your blouse," she said.

"Thanks." It was white with a pink monogram Granny Reeb had stitched. "Has anybody in your family ever died?" I asked her.

"Died?" Cathy looked incredulous.

"Yes, you know, stopped breathing, had to be put in the ground—"

"Sumi!" It was Mrs. Scott, from down at the end of the table. "Let's talk about something more appropriate, shall we?"

I guess death isn't appropriate.

"My aunt died," Jan put in. "She was murdered in a liquor store."

"Did you know her?"

"Well, sort of. It was way off in Oregon. She'd moved out there with her husband and gotten a job and there was this holdup. . . . They brought her home, though. Mama fainted at the funeral."

"People don't die in my family," Cathy said quietly. "At least not yet."

I don't know why that struck me as funny, but I laughed till I got the hiccups, then choked on water and laughed some more. Other kids sitting near us joined in. Maybe they were laughing at me, but I didn't care. "Immortal Blanchard!" I snorted.

The bell rang. Lunch hour wasn't over; it meant the next shift was headed in. I followed Cathy as she took her tray back. "I'm sorry," I said. "I didn't mean to make fun."

She looked surprised. "It *was* pretty funny. But I'd never thought of it, you know, nobody dying. . . . Now I'm worried."

"Are your grandparents old?"

"Not *that* old," she began, and for the rest of the

lunch hour we stood by the swings and she told me about her family. Once Ollie came by, stopped in front of us, and blurted, "I had a brother that shot his fool self."

"Did you know that?" I asked Cathy after he was gone.

"No. It must have been hushed up."

Then Ollie swaggered back. "Didn't die," he told us.

"My grandfather did."

"I'm sorry," Cathy said.

Then somebody came out and rang the bell. You can't hear the electric bells on the playground, so some seventh grader always has that job. I remember how proud I was when Drake did it.

"Did you know my brother went away to prep school?" I asked Cathy as we started in.

"I knew he went somewhere. Does he like it?"

"Oh, yeah. He's studying music."

"I guess he's all grown up now."

"Well, about half," I told her. "Like us."

# 24

MRS. SCOTT had to go to the dentist and we had a substitute that afternoon. Mrs. Day assigned us six math pages, four of which we'd already done. Nobody told her.

Slow as I am with numbers, I was finished long before class time was up. I sat looking at my paper. Fractions made me think of time signatures in my music books, of all the practicing I had done on piano and flute. Flute seemed hopeless but I wasn't too bad on piano. The trouble was, piano didn't appeal to me. What I really wanted to play was guitar. But my parents would think that was silly. I already had the flute and I'd been playing piano for years. No point in thinking about that.

I wandered over to the bookshelf. The book I pulled out was the same ragged one I'd looked at the day Cathy and I did the turkeys. It opened to the same page. I saw why. Someone had stuck the flap from a box of Milk Duds in there.

It was full spring now. Out the classroom window, dogwood bloomed pink and white against the incinerator. But the girl in the book still stared through her window into red leaves:

> Margaret, are you grieving
> Over Goldengrove unleaving?

My eyes felt hot and a shiver dropped over me like a net.

> Leaves, like the things of man, you
> With your fresh thoughts care for, can you?

The girl in the book wasn't crying. It must be me, my tears blurring the window. Why wouldn't Mother talk to me? What was I going to do?

Putting the book back, I remembered the first time I had read the poem. It had made me hot all over then, too, and I thought I was getting sick. Ha! It was what the poem knew that gave me a fever. I was coming down with life.

I looked at my classmates. Rose was writing a note, probably to Jimmy about Jan. Angie was filing her nails. Ollie was eating Twinkies behind his book. They all seemed perfectly at home.

Red Rover, Red Rover—

I remembered their voices chanting. How could I get over to where they were?

The day Mrs. Waltz took me from the playground, I thought she was the one. She would set the world right. But how could she? I couldn't tell her what was wrong. Any more than I could march into her room now and say, "Okay, periods mean you can have babies, but how?"

That wasn't the question anyway, not the main question. Facts would just be the beginning. Why had I lived happy and whole till this year when it all fell apart? Was it because Drake left? Because Papa Gene died? Because I started paying attention?

I was working on this when *bam!* an eraser hit me in the head, and the Saylor twins got sent to the principal.

"Everybody to their seats!" Mrs. Day was offended at having to raise her voice. Ollie stuffed the last Twinkie in his mouth.

"Now children," she began.

Not now, I wanted to say. We're not really children now. We've crossed over. You can make us sit in rows but you can't protect us. You can turn on all the lights but the shadows stick to us like skin.

"Take the spelling words on page 116 and use them in a letter. Be sure you write neatly and underline each one."

"Mrs. Scott never makes us do that," Jimmy complained.

"Then this is your chance to learn something new," Mrs. Day replied.

He shrugged. Oh, boy. I opened *My Word Book*. I hadn't written any letters since winter, had even given up on my diary. Why? I hadn't answered Keezie's postcard. What kind of friend was that?

I looked at the list of green words on the cloudy white page. Somebody had sweated on this book.

> enhance
> transport
> memorandum

Not the way to start with Keezie. I'd have some explaining to do. But what about Drake? He loved to play with words. He'd get a kick out of such a letter. If I hurried, I could make an extra copy in case Mrs. Day took this up. So I began:

*May 3rd*

*Dear Drake,*

*Please disregard all those letters I never sent you. I have been experiencing some difficulty in communication. It has been disorienting.*

*In accord with our previous arrangement, please come home soon so we can enhance a summer of transport.*

*This memorandum is intended to inform you that the Cave system is operational despite your absence, but your presence at home will be greatly appreciated.*

*Love,*
*Sumi*

I didn't know how you *enhance* a summer either, but Drake would have a theory. He'd be home in a month. In the meantime, he'd have this letter. It wouldn't join my rubber-banded stack. I'd fold it, put it in a paper pocket, stick on a president, and send it forth.

# 25

IT FELT GOOD, slipping that letter through the slot of the post office. Like I'd let go of something, taken off a heavy pack. Summer was almost here. Drake would come home. Granny Reeb would be back on Memorial Day. Maybe Keezie would come to visit! And I would close the door on this year.

Furthermore, there were summer doors I could open: diving lessons, reading projects, and maybe even teaching myself to play guitar. It occurred to me that I could try one of Daddy's own lines of persuasion: "If it was one mistake to start out on the flute," I would tell him, "it would be two mistakes to keep going." As for the money, I thought the music company might let me swap my flute. I took it in the next Saturday.

"Nice instrument," the clerk said. "How long have you had it?"

"Just nine months. I got it second-hand."

"And did it come from us?"

"Oh, yes. I meant to say that."

He gave a cautious smile, but there was more humor in his eyes.

"Very well. I'll have to ask Mr. Sturgill. Give me a few minutes."

He walked away, carrying the open flute case like a butterfly. I watched his thin back, the long pipes of his arms and legs. Something about that sight made my throat hurt, my eyes sting. He slipped into the office like the letter in that slot and I knew: he was built just like Papa Gene, had the same narrow shoulders, slender hands. *Can you touch your elbows behind your back?* I wondered. *Can you chin yourself with one hand?*

Blinking back tears, I turned to the music section. Piano, piano, drum, organ, guitar. There it was—a whole row of guitar books. Classical, folk, rock. I'd hoped for a Peter, Paul and Mary one, but didn't see any. The best choice looked to be *Beginning Folk Guitar*. I was flipping through it when the young man cleared his throat.

"Miss?"

I walked back to the counter.

"Mr. Sturgill said a trade would be fine, but the terms will depend on the instrument. Do you have one in mind?"

I didn't, but I knew which one as soon as he showed me the stock. It was small, maple-topped, a Regal steel-string. He lifted it down from the pegboard for me to try.

"I've never even *held* a guitar," I told him.

"Well," he said, "it's somewhat more fragile than a baby. On the other hand—" he was really smiling now—"you don't have to worry about it crawling away."

"You must have one," I said.

"A guitar?"

"No. A baby."

"That's right. And a guitar too. Mine is classical. See this F-6 Martin? Mine is very close in design, though I think its tone is better. Now let's hear the one you have."

I held the guitar gently and ran my thumb down across the strings. I wasn't even making a chord and it was thrilling.

"That's wonderful!" I told him.

"The D string's a bit flat but overall it does sound good. That guitar has a fine resonance. Try chording it, though. You need to get the feel of the fretboard and see how it fits your hand."

And right then and there he showed me how to make a G chord.

Fifteen minutes later, with grooves of pain on my fingertips, I handed the guitar back.

"How much does it cost?" I asked him.

"Seventy dollars and your flute."

"Oh. I'll have to talk to my parents."

"Of course."

But by the time I got home, Mr. Sturgill had already called. It turned out he owed Daddy money on a vet bill for his son's horse. And he offered to settle that debt with my trade.

"Can I do it? Can we do it?" I was all but jumping up and down.

"I don't see why not," Daddy said. "What do you think, Ivalea?"

"But she's just started the flute," Mother reminded him.

"Yes, but she hasn't gotten very far."

"That's true," Mother said. "I haven't heard anything resembling 'The Star-Spangled Banner.' " She smiled at us both and I realized I hadn't seen her that happy all year.

So it was settled, and on Monday after school I made the trade. The same clerk waited on me and, as a favor, offered to write out chords to a song I wanted to learn.

"*If* I know it," he said. "That's a big *if*."

I had to think fast. "How about '500 Miles'? It's a Peter, Paul and Mary song."

"Good! That's an easy one." And he got a white paper bag and wrote it out.

Only four chords, the whole song had only four chords! If I practiced hard enough I might be able to play it at the Memorial Day picnic. Sing it, even. No, maybe that was going too far. But I would try. I would give it my best effort. That was one thing about Drake and me: we were good workers. Not the same kind, but good nonetheless.

# 26

I SWEAR it didn't hit me till the next morning that I didn't have a flute to take to band.

"Oh, no," Mother said when I told her at breakfast. "I can't believe we did this." She was smiling though. "It reminds me of Uncle Eb when I was about your age."

"Why?" She was raining Total, like fall leaves, down from the box.

"Well, he'd just learned to drive and he went to the service station to fill up the car . . ." She paused, laughing. She hadn't done her hair yet and it hung gold around her shoulders, making her look like a girl. An old girl.

"But what's funny about that?"

"He was on his bicycle!" She was really laughing now and I had to laugh, too, at the image of Uncle Eb, straddling his two-wheeler and calling out, "Fill 'er up!"

Mother poured us some coffee and sat down.

"But what will Mr. Hanson say?" He's the band director. "I suppose Jeb Sturgill might let us borrow the flute back."

At this we both started laughing again. What had come over her? Or was it that something had been lifted off? *Like when I mailed the letter*, I thought. She'd been more herself ever since we saw Dr. Goss. Maybe it helped, too, that Granny Reeb was gone. For a while, at least, she didn't have that grief to tend to. Maybe that gave some room for her own.

Was grief what this year had been meaning? And had we borrowed each other's like a shawl? And was it lifted now, like the mantle of snow on the mountain, or unraveled into a hundred singing creeks?

"Guess what!" I said. "I'm going to sing at the picnic."

"Good." She looked startled.

"I mean I'm going to sing and play the *guitar*," I told her.

"In three weeks?"

"Yes ma'am."

"Then we better hold onto that guitar."

AS IT turned out, Mr. Hanson had given up on my flute career long before I had. When I explained my dilemma he just chuckled, rubbing his bearded chin with the palm of his hand.

"I'll tell you what," he began, leaning toward me. "If you bring that guitar and come to class every day, I'll let you practice in my office."

I was amazed. "That's terrific! Thank you."

"On one condition."

*Oh, dear*, I thought. *Here it comes.*

"You'll have to let me tell the class your circumstances. Otherwise we'll have a spring crop of kazoos, bongos, and bagpipes, and the parents will have my head if I try to say no."

I didn't like the idea, but I could see his point.

"Okay," I said.


SO THAT'S HOW I got to this minute, with new calluses on my fingers and my guitar shut up in the trunk. I told Drake my plan as soon as he got home.

"So you really took to Wendy's record?" he said. "That's great."

"Do you like it any more than you did?"

"It's nice, Sumi. It's just that the music's so simple. . . ."

"Simple is what I need."

A year ago I wouldn't have had this talk with Drake. Anything I thought he'd think silly I kept to myself. But now I look at him, taller and broadershouldered than when he left, having given up baseball cards and taken up bridge, and I realize he's *Drake*, he's not me. It's my voice I sing with, my skinny hands that make the chords. That's a funny thing, you know. Even when I was fat my hands were skinny—long and skinny, like Drake's. And Papa Gene's.

Now we're at the gate of Steep Stone Park. Granny Reeb will be here, brought home by Aunt Debbie and Uncle Hal. Aunt Jenny will bring Marvin and Brenda, her two. Nobody's sure when Uncle Eb and his bunch will make it. He had to work late, but they'll be here as quick as they can.

I wonder if Brenda will still do gymnastics, if Marvin will have outgrown his magic tricks. Drake isn't going to be in the Show this year. Says he's too old. Not me. I'm just beginning. I'll tune up and when it's my turn to stand in the light—from a car this year, Granny Reeb sold the jeep—I'll play the only four chords I know and sing:

Lord I'm one, Lord I'm two
Lord I'm three, Lord I'm four
Lord I'm five hundred miles
From my home.

Not a shirt on my back
Not a penny to my name . . .

I can sing it because I *am* home, for a while anyway, like Drake. And I'm looking for a life to take with me when I go.